RUTHLESS KINGDOM

BONEYARD KINGS #3

BECCA STEELE

C. LYMARI

Ruthless Kingdom

Copyright © 2022 by Becca Steele & C. Lymari

All rights reserved. No part of this book may be reproduced or transmitted in any form or by any means, electronic or mechanical, including photocopying, recording or by any information storage and retrieval system, without written permission from the author, except for the use of brief quotations in a book review.

Editing by Rumi

This is a work of fiction. Names, characters, businesses, places, events, locales, and incidents are either the products of the author's crazy imagination or used in a fictitious manner. Any resemblance to actual persons, living or dead, or actual events is purely coincidental.

SYNOPSIS

Bad things happened in threes, but they turned out to be a blessing in disguise. There was no escape from the Boneyard Kings, but now we're on the same side.

Our enemies came, but we didn't let them break us. They thought they could take us down, but they underestimated our strength.

Now, three rivals stand against three kings and their queen, and they're about to see just how ruthless our kingdom can be.
The game of chess is in play, and only one side can claim victory.
Who will be the one to call checkmate?

*To Rumi, who had to deal with us being last minute AF, and still managed to get our BonerRyard boys out on time.
You're the real MVP.*

PROLOGUE

There once was a kingdom built on blood, flesh, and bones. The people were good, but the rulers were cold. Money was power, and corruption brought gold. This empire was powerful, and no one dared disturb the throne.

Then one day, its rulers made not one, but two mistakes that brought forward a whole new game.

In the shadows, new alliances were made, and three little orphans learned the plays. They discovered horrors and uncovered lies. Still, every night, they asked themselves, "Why?"

No matter how close they got to the truth, something was missing. The most important clue. Rivers of blood flowed through their town, and they vowed to expose the culprits somehow.

They made their home a boneyard, built their kingdom on top, and crafted their crowns with metal to match.

But what was chess without its queen; except they never expected her to have three kings. So now the game comes to an end.

Who will be the one to call checkmate?

1

SAINT

They say your life flashes right before your eyes just as you are about to die. I felt like I had lived years in just a few short seconds. My eyes burned from trying to see more than I could in the dark. Warmth spread over my body, hyperaware of the blood running through my veins. My heart skipped a few beats, my chest feeling hollow and weak.

Fuck.

My legs were shaking, and I felt like I would fall to the ground. This was not how I envisioned tonight going.

I finally blinked, and my eyes felt some relief. When I opened them again, my surroundings had gotten brighter, but my hearing had faded.

How did things go so horribly wrong?

The woods seemed to come to life. The wind blew on the leaves, all of them witnessing the scene. How much time had passed? My ears still rang from being so close to the gun.

"Nothing a bullet can't fix."

Callum jumped into action while I stayed unmoving.

"*Fuck*... Hold the wound," he yelled. I blinked, and when I opened my eyes, Callum's hands were covered in blood. I never knew blood could be so bright and red. He was so pale, so maybe that's why the blood looked staggering against his skin.

I opened my mouth, but no words came out.

"Turn him on his side," Mateo barked.

His face was like stone. No emotions whatsoever, and that was what scared me the most. Death was in the air tonight, wasn't it? Someone was not coming out of these woods alive. We had been too naïve to think otherwise.

"Not yet. He's not breathing." Callum started to do compressions, and for once, I was glad he always had a clear head. I turned my head, and my eyes made contact with Lorenzo, and I couldn't do anything, just stay motionless. A smirk curved over his lips, and my body was on overdrive, that I didn't even feel myself shiver.

"What the fuck did this accomplish?" Callum seethed as he pushed his hands up and down. More blood soaked them. I wondered if the warmth of the blood bothered him.

Lorenzo's smirk turned into a full-blown smile. He walked closer and then put his hand on my shoulder and squeezed.

"Now we are all in this together," he spoke with a cheery bravado.

I took a deep breath, and it burned my lungs—kind of like when I was swimming. Denying air to my lungs for a short period did that.

"So this was your plan all along?" Mateo spoke in a deadly calm voice, and the last few seconds replayed all over again.

. . .

With every step deeper into the woods, unease spread through me. I turned to look at my brothers, and I knew they were thinking the same thing. When we saw Lorenzo, all of us were on our guard, prepared for his next move, and we forgot to keep an eye on what Rigo was doing.

The moment Lorenzo pulled the trigger, I couldn't blink. I felt that I would miss what would come next if I did. It was going to be either Mateo or me. Callum was on the other side, and I thanked God. He was out of harm's way. The bullet moved fast, but somehow, I could follow its trajectory. I turned my head as the bullet passed me until I saw the two people behind us.

The man next to Rigo staggered as the bullet made its impact. His hand came up to cover the place where the bullet had hit. He wore a white button-up shirt that quickly began to turn red.

Fuck.

Nothing a bullet couldn't fix, right?

Suddenly, Lorenzo's words made all the sense. Nothing said "we are on an even playing field" like being accessories to murder.

I waited for Lorenzo's answer, and he simply shrugged. "I'd say we are even now, wouldn't you?"

Callum cast a side-look at Lorenzo, but his focus was on the man lying on the ground. Mateo had turned him to see if the bullet had made an exit, but his back was clear of red.

I shook my head and sprang into action. For a few seconds, I was sure that bullet was meant for one of us. And now, I felt guilty that someone else was paying the price for the loyalty Lorenzo wanted us to have.

I kneeled next to Callum, blinking furiously to ensure that my vision did not fail me. The man whose blood Cal had on his arms couldn't be that of Robert Parker-

Pennington Sr. There was no way Lorenzo was that fucking insane.

"He's going to die unless we get him help," Mateo barked at Lorenzo, while Callum did everything he could to help the mayor stay alive.

Lorenzo nodded to Rigo, and he just nodded in return. I watched Callum and the mayor so intently, that I missed the moment Lorenzo came to me. He took my arm, and I watched as he put the gun in my hand, forcing me to grip it, ensuring my fingertips were all over it. Then he took it away with a rag.

Everything felt cold, and I knew Callum and Mateo were about to blow.

"So we're all going to kill the mayor, is that it?" I asked. "And to make sure none of us snitch, you'll keep the missing piece, so if we ever step out of line, the blame will be on me?"

I was pissed.

Lorenzo stepped closer and looked down at the mayor with disgust. "Nah, he can still be of some use to me."

"You're going to save him, just to use him?" Callum spoke. "Why not just threaten him?"

Rigo bent and started to carry the mayor as Callum helped.

"I didn't want him to think I was all bark and no bite."

With those words, we silently loaded the mayor into their car.

2

EVERLY

"Hello, Everly. I've been waiting for you."

The words rang in my ears as I met the gaze of the tall man with the dark, swept-back hair, heavyset brows, and a crooked nose. "I suppose I should introduce myself. Commissioner Peterson, chief of police." He lifted his hand, something metallic gleaming in his clenched fist.

Handcuffs.

"Be a good girl, and I won't have to use these on you." He spoke with no inflection in his tone, and I suddenly became aware of just how dangerous my position was. The chief of police had me. No one knew where I was, other than Lacey, my uncle's maid, who was fearful and desperate to get away. This wasn't my uncle. This man was an unknown entity.

Calling on every ounce of strength I possessed, I straightened up in my chair, and stared him down. "You were waiting for me? How did you know I'd be coming here?"

A smile curved over his lips, and it chilled me to the bone. "Humans are rather predictable. In my years in law enforcement, I've become somewhat familiar with patterns of behavior. After I received a call from your uncle to inform me that he had you locked in his study, followed by another call to tell me that the security guard had witnessed a girl being driven away by one of the members of staff, well..." He shrugged. "It was simple enough. I'm sure the maid informed you that her cousin holds a position of employment at the station."

Internally, I groaned. I should have remained in the car. This was my fault.

A horrible thought struck me. "What will happen to Lacey?"

"The girl who brought you in?" His tongue darted out to lick his lips, and he leered at me. I could barely contain my shiver of revulsion. "She is rather pretty, isn't she? I can see why Martin was so keen to keep her employed."

Fuck. You couldn't trust anyone in this city.

"Please, don't..."

Steepling his fingers, he raised a brow. "I don't think you're in a position to be negotiating, Miss Walker. But perhaps..." A thoughtful look came over his face. "Why don't you share with me just what you were hoping to discover in your uncle's study, and we can see about letting the girl go."

"You let her go, *then* I'll tell you." Holding my composure was the hardest thing I'd ever had to do. My trembling hands were hidden in my lap, out of sight, and I had no doubt that this man would seize on any perceived weakness, scenting it like a shark with blood in the water.

This time, he gave me what appeared to be a genuine smile. "A spine of steel. I like that. Your uncle has taught you well."

"Do we have a deal?" I asked, instead of responding to his comment.

"The girl is inconsequential. You have a deal, *if* the information you give me is satisfactory. I'm afraid I can't let her leave before then."

What should I tell him that would satisfy him? My uncle had probably already told him everything that had happened, but I needed to be careful not to reveal anything other than what my uncle already knew. "I was in his study. I'd gone in there to look for more family photos—we'd been looking at them earlier that evening. He'd fallen asleep, and I didn't think he'd mind. Then..." The sudden tremble in my voice wasn't even faked as I recalled how he'd stormed into the study, yanking me around and screaming in my face. I'd never seen him like that before. He'd always been so controlled. "Then he came bursting in, ranting about residue in his glass, and shouting about me going to the ball and something about the junkyard. I thought he was drunk, or on drugs, or something. I've never seen him act that way before."

Tears filled my eyes as I allowed my very real fear to surface. Something flashed in the police chief's gaze, a second of uncertainty, and I pressed home my advantage. With a wobble in my voice, I continued, "He locked me in his study and left me there. Why would he do that to his own niece?"

Commissioner Peterson's mouth thinned. "Perhaps we should continue this interview after I've spoken to your uncle again."

"Can I leave?"

He laughed humorlessly. "That won't be possible, I'm afraid."

"You can't just hold me here against my will! I'm not a suspect! This must be against the law!"

"Miss Walker. Have you forgotten who I am? I *am* the law."

I didn't know how much time had passed, because there wasn't a clock in the interrogation room, but by the time the sound of the door unlocking echoed through the small space, my throat was bone dry from lack of water, and I was starting to feel light-headed and sleepy. This wasn't good—I needed to be on alert.

Straightening up in my seat, I rubbed at my eyes and attempted to clear my throat, mentally preparing myself for another round of questions.

But that wasn't what happened. Instead of the chief of police, my uncle filled the doorway, a dark look on his face as he met my eyes.

Fuck.

He stepped into the room, and closed his hand around my bicep, his grip hard and bruising. "You're coming with me."

All I could do was stumble along with him as he hustled me down a long corridor, around a corner, and out of a door. The night air hit me, and I took a deep, gulping breath.

Wait. I was *outside*. And there was no one else around that I could see.

Taking my chances, I suddenly dropped my weight and twisted. My uncle, unprepared, stumbled forward, his grip on my arm loosening, and I tore myself away from him and ran.

My lungs were burning, and the sound of my shoes on

the asphalt was loud in the quiet night. I pushed forward, gasping for air, aiming in the direction of the road.

I had a sudden sense of déjà vu, except when I'd run from the Boneyard Kings, I hadn't been this scared.

Fuck, I wished they were here. But they weren't, and it was up to me to save myself.

Almost there.

A voice rang out in the darkness, loud and commanding.

"Stop, or I'll shoot."

I pushed forward.

A shot sounded, a burst of noise that rebounded off the buildings. There was a resounding, metallic crack as the bullet embedded itself into the side of the parked car I was passing right at that moment.

"Final warning."

A sob tore from my throat before I could stop it. I came to a halt, gasping for breath, tears of frustration and despair gathering in my eyes.

When I turned around, the chief of police was there with his gun trained on me, and my uncle was next to him, his face a mask of cold fury.

"You made a big mistake, Everly," my uncle ground out. "A very big mistake."

Then he yanked my arms behind my back, and cuffs were clicked into place on my wrists. When I opened my mouth to scream, the gun was pressed to my temple. My whole body trembled as I was picked up by Commissioner Peterson, bound and helpless, and carried to a dark, hidden part of the parking lot.

A nondescript van was parked there, and my uncle unlocked the doors. Everything in me wanted to struggle, but the cold metal of the gun was still pressed against me, and I had the feeling that the chief of police wouldn't hesitate to shoot.

I was pushed inside the van, and dark, rough fabric brushed against my cheek. It had obscured most of my vision before I registered that it was a bag being placed over my head.

Then the doors slammed, and the van started up.

3

MATEO

Never in a million years did I think I would be praying for the mayor not to fucking die. I couldn't care less about him—but I did care for Saint. If the dear old mayor died before we got him help, his death would be hanging over our heads. Lorenzo would forever hold the missing piece that killed him.

Lorenzo and Rigo drove at a normal speed while Callum kept the pressure on the wound steady to try and control the amount of blood loss. Saint looked out the window, probably cursing Callum and me. We shouldn't have gotten into bed with Lorenzo, and now it was too late.

Fuck.

"Where are we going?"

"Ay tranquilo, compa, hoy no vine la muerte." With ease, *brother, death won't be coming today,* Rigo responded nonchalantly. I shook my head, keeping my rage in check. They were clearly unhinged, and nothing I said would be beneficial at this moment.

We were back on the outskirts of town when they made a turn into some old factories. The garage attached to one of them opened as soon as we were in front of it. Two of Lorenzo's men waited at the front as we parked.

When the car stopped, Saint jumped out, and I quickly followed. Callum stayed put because he needed the mayor stable, and minimum movement was key so he wouldn't bleed out.

"Where's the doc?" Lorenzo asked as he got out of the car.

The men who had been waiting nodded toward the door. And we knew that we had to take the mayor there and hope that it wasn't too late, despite what Rigo had suggested.

We carried the mayor inside the warehouse between Callum and me, to where the doctor was waiting. There was nowhere to put him other than on top of a billiard table.

"What's the issue?" the "doc" asked.

"He's been shot," Callum deadpanned as he raised his bloody hands. He looked like something straight out of *Carrie* that I would have laughed at if the situation wasn't so dire.

The doc nodded as he put on latex gloves and got to work. The three of us took a step back to give him some room to work.

Saint went to the other side of Callum and put his hand on his shoulder. "Prom?"

I couldn't help snickering at his dumb as fuck remark. Callum shook his head, but there was a smirk on his face. I knew that it wasn't just me that had started to breathe easier.

"It won't be a perfect job," the man said.

"Will he live?" Lorenzo replied, unbothered.

"Yes," the man said confidently.

"Go for it," Lorenzo dismissively said.

The man nodded, then Lorenzo said something to Rigo and left the room with the Glock alongside him.

"You," the man turned around and looked at Saint. "Get me some water and a rag."

Saint looked around, a little confused since he wasn't one of Lorenzo's men. Callum pointed to the end of the room where a sink was located.

"Better get to work, Nurse Devin."

He looked a bit confused but started to do as the man was instructing him. We pulled up to the other side of the billiard table and watched as they removed the man's shirt. Blood was starting to soak more of the mayor's abdomen. When the so-called doctor began to touch the wounded area, he groaned.

One of the men who had been outside came in holding a bottle of tequila. The man accepted it and took a swig from it. I sighed. The mayor had so much, and he'd ended up with a back-alley surgery. Karma at its finest. I couldn't bring myself to feel sorry for him. We all made our bed and had to lie in it. His was covered in piss and shit.

After the man had gotten his drink in, he poured some on the wound. The mayor screamed.

"Hold him down!" the man instructed Saint.

Saint's hands came to the mayor's shoulders, trying to push him back down to the table without touching the affected area.

"I'm going to remove the bullet, then I want you to add pressure on the wound, got it?"

Saint nodded as the man took two long tweezer-like instruments from his bag. He dropped some tequila on them and then did as he had said.

The mayor's screams were so high-pitched and whiny at this point that the other men started to laugh.

"No que muy macho?" Rigo boasted. And it was something I could agree on. The mayor was doing shit up and down in this town, but he was barely handling the dose of his own medicine when it came to himself.

The so-called doctor pulled the bullet out and put it on top of the table while Saint added pressure to the wound. He then went back to his bag and pulled out the stuff necessary to stitch the wound closed. We all watched as he worked fast and calmly as the mayor whined.

"He will be fine," the man said, and we all sighed in relief. "These should help with the pain, and make sure he stays hydrated. Anything comes up, call my burner."

He directed his attention to Rigo. He nodded and then got up, handing him a wad of cash. The man greedily took it and left without looking back.

"So, now what?" Saint asked as he looked at the blood on his hands.

"Now we wait for the good old mayor to cooperate."

The mayor had his eyes closed, probably too tired from crying out. With another nod, the man who had been waiting outside for us went to pick him up.

"Put him in a room, and don't let him die."

"Are we free to go?" Callum asked.

Rigo looked at the three of us and smiled.

"I'll have someone take you back to your truck."

"Thanks," I said as the three of us started to walk out.

Once outside, I noticed just how late it was. Saint pulled up his phone and scrunched his brows as he looked at the screen.

"What's wrong?" Callum asked.

"Everly didn't try to contact us at all," he said, sounding disappointed.

"'Cause you're annoying," I joked as Callum pulled his phone out and put it to his ear.

"She's not answering," he said a few seconds later.

We all looked at each other but didn't say more because the guy giving us a ride had come out. The drive back to the truck was fucking slow, but one thing was for sure, none of us liked the radio silence coming from her.

4

EVERLY

I wasn't aware of how much time had passed when we finally came to a stop. I'd wedged myself into a corner of the van, bracing my body against two of the sides so I didn't overbalance, after we'd taken the first corner too sharply and I'd smacked my head against the metal.

The doors opened with a screech, and hands tugged me out of the van. I shivered a little as the cool night air hit my skin, although my face was hidden from the elements, thanks to the bag still covering my head. My cuffs were removed, and I desperately wanted to rub at my sore wrists, but I was being held too tightly. As I was manhandled away from the van, what felt like small pebbles crunched under my feet. I thought I heard the caw of a crow, but I might have been mistaken.

There was a sound of creaking wood, and my foot hit something raised. I fell to my hands and knees before anyone could catch me, skidding along, my palms grazing cold, worn stone.

"Get up," a voice hissed. It sounded like my uncle

although my senses were dulled, thanks to the thick material covering my head. A hand yanked me upright, jerking my arm painfully, and I bit back a cry of pain. No matter what, I wouldn't give them a reaction. It was only a tiny act of rebellion, but it was my way to stay strong, to retain some control even though my current situation wasn't looking good.

I was dragged along a little way, and then we made a turn. Pulled to a sudden stop, I stumbled again, but this time an arm grabbed me around my waist, fingers digging into my skin.

"Don't move," the same voice threatened.

The next second, a noise echoed through the space. Stone scraping on stone, loud and jarring. It felt like it went on forever—until it abruptly stopped, with the sound still ringing in my ears.

A hand pushed down on my head, and then I was led forward.

Stairs.

We went down.

And down.

I counted seventeen steps in all.

Even through the bag, I could tell that the air was different down here. Musty and stale. There was an oppressive feel to the space, and as soon as the bag was ripped from my head, I understood why.

We were underground. Thick stone walls surrounded me, and all around me were huge, rectangular objects, carved from stone, illuminated by a dozen candles placed around the space, wax dripping down the sides and pooling below, suggesting they'd been lit for some time before we got here. Was this where my uncle had been before he showed up at the police station? Where exactly were we?

I finally realized what the rectangular objects were.

Coffins.

I was in a crypt.

My hand went to my mouth, as my brain struggled to comprehend what I was seeing.

"Speechless, Miss Walker?"

My gaze snapped to the chief of police, who gave me a sardonic smile from his position in front of the stairs. In the flickering candlelight, shadows danced around him, making him look sinister and deadly. The light caught on the gleam of the gun barrel as he casually polished it on the sleeve of his coat, never taking his eyes from mine.

"Where—" My voice came out as a cracked rasp, so I cleared my throat, and tried again, fisting my hands to hide their tremble. "Where are we? What do you want with me?"

I'd been so focused on Commissioner Peterson that I hadn't even noticed my uncle until he was right behind me, twisting my arms behind my back. Before I could move, he was binding me with thick, heavy rope, so tight that I couldn't move.

He spoke low in my ear. "I'm sorry, Everly. I wish I didn't have to do this, but you brought this on yourself when you betrayed me."

"I didn't betray you. I don't know what you're talking about. Please, let me go!" I allowed the fear to surface once more, and tears filled my eyes effortlessly. I was truly scared, fearful of what they might do to me, but I would do whatever I could to make them believe I was innocent.

"Martin, maybe—"

"We talked about this!" My uncle's harsh tone left no room for argument. To my surprise, I saw Commissioner Peterson merely nod in acquiescence.

"As you wish." He took a step back, up onto the bottom

stair that led back to the surface level. Raising his voice, he addressed me. "Maybe some time spent here alone to reflect on things might help you to remember what you were doing earlier this evening."

"Please, don't leave me here," I begged in a whisper, lunging forward. I instantly realized that there was nowhere I could go. I'd been bound to something behind me, and I was unable to move.

My uncle strode past me, joining the chief of police at the foot of the stairs. "We'll be back tomorrow, Everly."

Then they both turned their backs on me and left. I heard the heavy scraping sound of the stone moving back into place, before I was plunged into silence, the thick stone stopping any other sounds from penetrating my prison.

I had to get free. I wasn't going to sit here and wait for them to come for me. Who knew what they might do if I continued to refuse to provide them with the answers they wanted to hear?

I desperately struggled against the ropes, hearing a clink as my ring fell to the floor. My breath caught in my throat, my eyes filling with tears. That ring meant everything to me.

Twisting as much as I could, I strained my eyes in the dim candlelight to see what I was tied to. It looked like the ropes had been looped several times around a large statue of a man that stood next to a huge coffin, both objects taking up their own space at one end of the crypt. With slow, careful movements, I managed to turn just about enough to be able to make out the coffin properly, feeling the rough bonds of the rope pulling at my skin as I did so.

Stretching as much as my bindings would let me, I reached out, tracing my bound fingers over the indentations in the stone. There was a name carved there.

Charles Blackstone.

The founder of Blackstone.

My panted breaths were loud in the stillness.

One by one, the candles flickered out, until there was only darkness.

5
SAINT

I was going out of mind. I kept looking down at my phone every five minutes to ensure it wasn't on silent mode. The house felt quiet as fuck—no one was saying anything. I was waiting for Callum to finish showering, since he was the one who had the most blood on him. We couldn't risk going anywhere with the mayor's blood on us.

"Anything?" Mateo asked as he came back, already in a new change of clothes.

I shook my head because, what else could I tell them? Deep in our guts, we knew something was wrong.

The bathroom door opened, and Callum came out wrapped in a towel.

"Put all your clothes in the bag," he said as he looked at me.

Without any words, I made my way to the bathroom. I removed all my clothes and put them in a black bag in the corner. The water was starting to get cold, and I finished up quickly.

"What the hell is going on?" My whisper echoed in the small bathroom.

I wrapped a towel around my waist and went to my room. Mateo was coming out of his room with a pile of clothes he had been wearing. When I moved, he took the garbage, threw his clothes in, and left to go outside to burn them.

We weren't going to risk anything.

Once I was dressed, I rejoined Callum and Mateo in the living room.

"Anything?" I asked, hoping that they knew something I didn't.

"We are going to her uncle's," Callum said.

"And do what?" I asked. "He hates us. He won't hesitate to call the cops on us—worse, do something to fuck our scholarships."

"Just to watch," Mateo stated.

I couldn't help but wonder—if I hadn't forced Everly to go with me to the ball, would things be a little different? Her uncle had hated that.

"You think her friends know anything?" was my next question.

"That's our next stop," Mateo said.

The drive to campus was quiet, with Callum and Mateo checking their phones as I drove. We stopped at Everly's dorm first.

"I swear to God if she's sleeping..." I mumbled as they made work to open her lock.

The room was empty. We knew it would be, but we had hoped.

"Time for the next stop," I sighed.

Hallie and Mia happened to be together, which made it easier to ask them simultaneously.

"I think it's better if I wait outside for this one," I said as we got to the building.

"Why?" Callum raised a brow.

I scratched my head.

"I might have offended Mia."

Mateo snorted.

"At least you didn't fuck them."

I flipped them off, and as soon as they left, I pulled out my phone and called Everly again. With every ring, my stomach sank further. This was a feeling I hated. It reminded me of the nights when I would be alone in the trailer while Tiff had men over. The anxiety would settle over me, wondering if she passed out if they would try to get handsy with me. When I was little, I dreaded her dying. Not because she was my mom, but because I didn't want to deal with being the one who found her.

Everly's phone rang two times, then I sat up straighter, thinking she had answered, but it went to voicemail. My heart sank. I immediately called again, and this time it didn't even ring. Her voicemail came on instantly.

Fuck.

I was pacing outside the car when Cal and Mateo came back. The grim look on their faces was enough to know Everly wasn't with her friends either.

"Do you think Lorenzo might have her?" was the first thing I asked, and it instantly put them on alert.

"Why?" Mateo asked.

"I called her again, and it rang two times before sending me to voicemail. Then I hung up and called again, and it turned off. It doesn't even ring anymore."

"No, I don't think he does. The mayor was more than enough for him," Callum said calmly, but the look on his face was anything but calm.

"Let's go," I barked.

The three of us got in the truck as Callum drove us away.

We were almost at her uncle's house when my phone began to ring. Hope swelled in my chest as reached for it. I always dreaded getting calls from Tiff, but today was not the day for her to fuck with me. I always felt some sort of guilt for ignoring her but pressing the End button was a relief today of all days.

"It's Tiff," I said, letting them know it wasn't Everly.

"You sure you don't want to get that?" Cal asked nonchalantly.

"Keep driving," I said, my tone harsh.

Right now, nothing mattered except Everly. Since I knew that she wasn't in her room, nor with her friends, I put my phone away because this was the last shred of hope we were holding on to.

We parked the truck a bit down the street from the dean's place. Getting out silently, we made our way to the back of the house.

"Stick to the shadows," Mateo said, as if we didn't know.

We moved stealthily through the dean's backyard. We were trying to get into the house through one of the side entrances when the knob started to move.

Shit.

We stepped back when the door opened, and we got ready for anything. At this point, the three of us were out of our minds. We would do what it took to get our girl back.

An elderly maid stood at the other end of the open door. Her eyes were widened when she saw us. She opened her mouth. Mateo was moving in an instant, grabbing her and turning her around with a hand to her mouth.

"We won't hurt you," Cal said soothingly. "We're looking for Everly."

She visibly relaxed.

"If he lets you go, can we trust you not to yell?" I asked.

She nodded her head immediately like it was no issue at all. Mateo removed his hand from her mouth and took a step back.

The lady looked at all of us and then moved back so she could be by the door. "You should leave," she said. "Ms. Walker isn't here."

"Where is she?" I demanded as I took a step forward.

The maid looked nervous, glancing behind her to see if anyone was coming. "She got in an altercation with Master, and she left."

Fuck—what did that mean? About what?

"What do you mean?"

"I can't say more," she said, taking a step back, trying to close the door.

I moved and put a hand to stop her from getting away.

"Please," I begged.

"I think she went to the station, but that would have been a mistake..."

She pulled her hand from my grasp and closed the door.

"Fuck," Callum said.

"This is some bullshit," Mateo added.

We hurried the fuck out of the rich side of town, toward the precinct, trying to figure out what the fuck was going on.

6

CALLUM

Of all the places she could've gone, I would've thought our girl would be smarter than to go to the cops, so there had to be more to it that we weren't aware of. Getting the cops involved was the opposite of what we wanted—sure, we had an in with some of them, but Everly's uncle and the mayor held more sway over those who were higher up.

"Here's what's going to happen." I pulled the truck to a stop a little way from the precinct, where we had a clear view of the parking lot and entrance. "This place is going to have security everywhere, so we need to play it safe for now. I'm going to go in and report a missing car. You know that one we switched the plates with, that favor we did for Lorenzo's buddy last month? They won't be able to trace anything, but it'll give us an excuse. You two, stay here for now. We can't afford to get caught poking around in places we shouldn't be." Rubbing my hand across my face, I sighed. "I have a gut feeling that Everly isn't here, but right now, this is our only lead, as much as I really fucking wish it wasn't."

"I'm not waiting here while you go off and play the

hero." Saint's mouth set in a flat line as he folded his arms across his chest.

Mateo looked between us, his brows pulled together. "Saint. He's right. We don't know what's happened, and if we don't stay low, we could be making shit worse for her."

"Fine. But if you're not back out here in ten minutes, I'm coming in." Saint jabbed a finger into my chest. I refrained from rolling my eyes, giving him a sharp nod.

"Deal. I'll be as quick as I can." With that, I climbed out of the truck, leaving the keys in the ignition in case they needed to make a quick getaway while I was inside.

Fuck. I hated coming here, but we needed to get our girl back, and fast. Alarm bells were blaring—the second the maid had mentioned an altercation between Everly and her uncle, I'd had a sick feeling in my stomach.

As soon as I was inside the building, I headed straight over to the guy at the desk. I didn't know him personally, but he was from our side of town, and I knew his name was Samuel. Which meant that I could probably intimidate him into talking if he needed an incentive. He glanced up from his computer screen, his eyes widening when he took me in.

"Wh-what do you want?" he stammered.

There was no one else in here, but I knew the cameras would be running. Making sure my voice carried, I leaned closer, tapping my fingers on the counter in a sign of impatience. "I need to report a missing vehicle."

He stared at me, frowning, but eventually nodded. "Okay. Lemme get the form."

When he slid the form in front of me, along with a pen, I lowered my voice. "Did a girl come in earlier?"

His eyes flicked to mine, comprehension dawning in his gaze. Then they narrowed. "What's the information worth?"

"Do you know who I am? That should be incentive enough."

"Y-yes. This information might have value, though."

When he spoke those words, it took everything in me to maintain my aloof façade. I gave him a slow nod, then glanced back down at the form, scribbling out the details of the supposedly missing vehicle. "I'm listening. If the information is satisfactory, I might be able to do you a deal. Take a bathroom break, or whatever excuse you need to make, and come and find me. I'll be parked down the street."

With that, I signed off the form, threw the pen down, and got out of there.

Back at the truck, I slid into the driver's seat, and put the truck into reverse, rolling it back down the street until it was out of sight of the precinct.

"Well? What happened?" Saint broke the silence.

"I might have something for us. Maybe. He—" I cut myself off as Samuel appeared on the sidewalk, jogging toward the truck. I made eye contact with him through the windshield and indicated for him to climb into the back.

"Oh, shit," he said, when he got in and realized that he had the attention of all three of the Boneyard Kings. "I'm too young to die."

"He's as dramatic as you, Saint," I commented dryly. Saint punched me in the arm, but I ignored him, giving Samuel my attention. "What can you tell us about the girl?"

His hands were shaking, but he held his head high and met my gaze head-on, which made me respect him. "She came in earlier with my cousin. My cousin was all shook up, wanting to report her employer—"

"Who's her employer?" Mateo voiced the question I'd been just about to ask, but I already knew the answer.

"Martin Walker." He gave a bitter smile. "Yeah, that asshole got handsy with her."

"This fucker needs to die," Saint muttered, and I agreed with him.

"She was filling in the forms when the chief came over. It was unusual because he never gets involved with any of the front desk shit. He asked her a few questions, and then said they'd need some details from the witness. He disappeared after that, and then Maura—she's a member of the admin team—spoke to my cousin. Next thing I knew, my cousin was bringing this girl in. Long, dark hair, big eyes, really nice—"

"Watch what you're saying. She's ours," I ground out, and his eyes widened.

"Uh. Really nice... shoes," he continued, doing his best to ignore Saint's snort of amusement. "Maura took her into one of the interrogation rooms, and I didn't think anything of it to begin with, because they sometimes do that, y'know? But then I saw the chief disappear in the same direction, and I knew there was something else going on."

"Is she still there?" My fists were clenched, and my jaw was so tight it was giving me a headache. The more I heard, the more worried I was for our girl.

He shook his head. "No. I don't know where she is, but I can give you a lead. But I want something in return."

"Of course you fucking do." Mateo rolled his eyes. "What do you want?"

"An in with Lorenzo. I want to fight in the ring."

We all glanced at each other. "Look. You seem like a good kid. You don't wanna get yourself mixed up with Lorenzo." Saint reached over to pat Samuel's shoulder, and he flinched away.

"Kid? I'm probably older than you, dude." He met my gaze again. "Those are my terms. Take them or leave them."

"Fine. You've got a deal. But you need to think long and hard about whether you want to go down that road. Once you get caught up in Lorenzo's web, there's no getting out." I was speaking from experience, and I knew that in his eyes, we were tight with Lorenzo, but I had to at least warn him what he was getting himself into. Hopefully Lorenzo wouldn't be interested in him anyway, but you never knew what was going on in his mind.

"Thank you." Samuel relaxed back against the seat. "It all went quiet for a while. I called my friend to pick up my cousin, and then I took a break. I was curious what the chief wanted with the girl. There was no sign of them, and I was just passing the back exit when I heard a gunshot. I ran to the door in time to see the chief and Martin Walker throwing the girl into the back of a white van, then they drove off."

"Fuck. Fuck, fuck, fuck!" I slammed my hands down on the dash. I wasn't one to lose my cool, but I was sick to my stomach thinking what might have happened to Everly.

"The gunshot... Was she okay?" Saint's voice was the quietest I'd ever heard it, and when I turned to look at him, his green eyes were suspiciously damp.

Samuel bit down on his lip. "I don't know. She was alive. But it was too dark to see much."

We were all on the verge of losing it, I could tell, and it was up to me to keep it together. Straightening up, I forced my nausea down and met Samuel's eyes. "What can you tell me about the van?"

He gave me a half smile, and for the first time, I had hope. "I can tell you that I got a good look at the plates when it was waiting to turn out of the parking lot. And I can also tell you that I ran them through the system, and I have the details of the van."

Finally.

We had a real, solid lead.

We'd get our girl back.

And if one hair on her head was harmed, there'd be hell to pay.

7

MATEO

It was like I could fucking breathe again. I didn't realize how tense I had been until the dipshit spoke up with information that could actually be of some use. When he began to talk, I was close to punching him, but Cal quickly controlled the situation. Like hell would someone speak about Everly like that in front of us.

"Are you prepared to die?" I asked the guy before he got out of the truck. He just stared at me with wide eyes—no one ever wanted to die. As humans, we feared death, so we didn't think of it. As if that made it not real. Death was a constant companion that stuck close when you lived in the gutters, so you never lost sight of what could happen with one wrong move. I knew it. My brothers did as well. And we knew no quick buck was worth it. Especially not with men like Lorenzo.

"If you want an in with Lorenzo, then you better be ready to die. You live by the sword. You gotta die by it too."

His face paled, and he got out without another word.

"I think you made him wet himself a bit," Saint joked. I

took that as a good sign, since he wasn't being an ass now that we had a lead on Everly.

"Dumb people like him are the first to get killed when they get tangled with men like Lorenzo."

None of them said otherwise because we all knew it was true. Between the three of us, we had yet to be able to get out of his grasp.

"Any idea on how we will find the van?" Saint asked.

Callum and I turned to look at each other, wicked grins spreading across our lips.

"What?" Saint questioned when we turned to look at him.

"We are the fucking Boneyard Kings for a reason," I said, and they agreed.

"Text all your contacts. Cash prize or favor for whoever finds that van first," Callum added as he began to furiously type.

We didn't want to ask Lorenzo for more favors, but we didn't need to when the people on our side of town would gladly do all the work for a shot at some cash or a favor from the kings. Things didn't look so grim right now.

"What do we do now?" Saint asked as he looked at his dead phone. We knew come tomorrow, after we found Everly, because there was no way in hell her dipshit uncle was taking her from us—come tomorrow, Saint would be flooded with his mom's shame.

"We wait," Callum said as he moved the truck. As soon as we started driving, raindrops began to hit the truck, getting heavier as time went by. This was going to be a bitch, but I had faith in the people of this town. I had faith that our girl was hanging tight because that was the thing about Everly—the more you tried to push her into a corner, the more she got the will to fight back. It was why she brought the three of us down to our fucking knees.

The streets were fucking dark as we drove through them.

"It feels like déjà vu," Saint said. "But with a truck."

It would have been funny if it wasn't a fucking traumatizing night for the three of us.

Just as he finished speaking, blue and red lights flashed behind us.

"Shit," Callum hissed.

"Did you forget the blinker?" Saint asked as Callum put the truck to a stop.

"I did nothing wrong," Cal replied as he put the truck in park and reached for his license, registration, and insurance.

We knew for sure all our lights were on. None of them had gone out on us. What kind of mechanics would we be if we didn't service our own vehicle to perfection?

"Let me do the talking," Cal told us as a man began to approach us.

One thing we were sure about was that we were being profiled. No way was this just a coincidence.

Only once the officer was at the window did Callum bring it down. "Did we do anything wrong, officer?" he asked before the cop could get a word in.

A bright light blinded us when the stupid pig flashed it in all of our faces.

"It's Chief," the cocksucker said arrogantly.

Yeah, this was connected with our girl.

"My apologies, *Chief*," Callum went on just as my cellphone pinged. "Is there a reason we got pulled over?"

Ignoring them, I opened my phone and saw that someone had seen the van and had given us a lead. I felt like an idiot for not going there on my own sooner, and I knew my brothers would too. We just needed to lose the tail now.

"Suspicious activity was reported around this area," he said distastefully.

I fisted my hands because it was always something with people like him, finding any excuse to oppress the people.

"Oh, I wasn't aware it was illegal to drive around," Callum added, and Saint snickered. I had to elbow him so we could be let go ASAP.

"It's not," the chief added as he flashed the light once again.

This time I turned around, glaring. Our gazes met, and something was familiar about him, but I couldn't put my finger on what it was. I cocked my head, trying to get a better look, but he turned off the flashlight.

"Get on home, it's not safe to be out this late," he stated, but it was more like a threat.

He handed Callum his license, insurance, and registration. As soon as he was away, Cal pulled the window up.

"Did he just threaten us?" Saint asked the obvious.

Ignoring his question and the nagging feeling that I knew that cocksucker, I looked at both of them and told them what the message said.

"Someone reported a van that fit the description by the old church."

"Fuck," Saint hissed.

"Now we have to get there without a tail," Cal added as he pulled away.

"Let's get our girl," I told them, hoping like hell she was okay, because if she wasn't, this town would pay.

8

CALLUM

Now wasn't the time to lose my cool. Everyone was counting on me, and I wouldn't let them down. I'd wanted to punch that smug fucker in the face, but I resisted—you didn't go around assaulting the chief of police unless you wanted to make life hell for yourself. We knew that he'd taken Everly, though, and that meant he was going to pay. Even if he wasn't involved in any of the other shit that Everly's uncle was into, he'd hurt our girl, and that meant there'd be repercussions.

But not yet. Right now, getting Everly was the only thing that mattered.

It became clear to me that we were being tailed, so I came up with a plan. It wasn't a great plan, but it was all I had, and time wasn't on our side. Taking a left instead of a right at the next exit, I headed back in the direction of the junkyard.

"What are you doing?" Saint hissed. "This isn't the way to the church."

Glancing in the rear-view mirror, I saw the car tailing us at a discreet distance had also turned left. "I know. We're being followed, so we need to shake them before we can get Everly."

Next to me, Mateo's jaw tightened. "Assholes."

"Yeah." Pulling up outside the junkyard, I left the truck to idle while Saint jumped out and opened the gates for us. As I drove the truck inside, I saw the car that had been following us drive past at a slow speed. When the gates clanged shut behind us, it sped up, disappearing into the distance.

I parked outside the house and turned to Mateo and Saint. "Here's what we're going to do. We leave the truck here. Saint, go in the house and turn the lights on, make it look like we're home. Mateo, come with me. We're gonna need to use Glenda."

They both groaned, like I knew they would. Hell, I didn't like this option, but it was the only one we had right now.

"Hey, boys, I want you to meet Glenda." The old man gave us a crooked grin, throwing out his hand. We exchanged glances. What the fuck was this old wreck of a sedan we were meant to be looking at, and why did he seem so pleased?

"Now, now, I know she ain't pretty to look at." He interpreted our glances correctly. "But ol' Glenda here, she was the first car I ever worked on. She was left here to die, and I brought her back to life. It took me hours of blood, sweat, and tears, but I fitted her with a new engine, tires, a cam belt... all parts from cars that no one wanted anymore. They used to dump them on this land, see, and that was when I had the idea of opening the junkyard."

Moving closer, he ran a hand lovingly over the rusted hood. "Call me sentimental, but we've been together from the beginning, and I don't want to change her. She's perfect just the way she is."

. . .

Glenda was in an even worse state than she had been then. Fuck, I didn't even know if she'd start—she was temperamental as fuck, and slow, too, but she was our only option. Mateo helped me to uncover her, then topped up her tank with one of the jerry cans we had stashed in the workshop, while I checked the oil and water levels. Satisfied that we'd at least be able to get her running, I grabbed the keys and slid into the driver's seat. At least it had stopped raining, because even her wiper blades were temperamental.

Without even needing to be asked, Mateo climbed into the back and lay low, where he wouldn't be spotted from outside. When Saint joined us, he did the same, both of them contorting themselves into the space. I prayed under my breath as I turned the key in the ignition, and after a couple of sputtering false starts, the engine came to life.

The car jerked as I backed her out of the covered storage area where we kept her, and I eased up on the gas. The engine coughed a few times, but didn't cut out, and all three of us breathed a sigh of relief when we were finally at the gates. I jumped out quickly to open them wide enough for the car to squeeze out, then ran to close them behind me.

Finally back in the car, I pointed it in the direction of the abandoned church. Time to go and get our girl.

It was painful, driving Glenda. I had to keep the needle at 30 mph or below, otherwise the steering wheel would start to shake, and the car would judder along, threatening to cut out. Thanks to our slow pace, it seemed to take forever to get to the church, but finally, we were there. I parked a little way from it, out of sight.

"I didn't see any cars in the parking lot," Mateo commented, straightening up from his cramped position. I was surprised he'd been able to see anything out of the window, he'd been lying so low.

"Yeah, me neither, but that doesn't mean there isn't someone here. We need to find Everly, and I'm not leaving until we've searched every inch of the place." Climbing out of the car, I turned to Saint. "Let's circle the outside first, then meet at the entrance if we don't find anything, yeah?"

Both of them slipped off, dark shadows in the night, and I did the same, completing my own circuit of the overgrown graveyard until I was sure that there was no one else around. That just left the inside of the small church.

The three of us entered the stone building silently. Mateo brought up his phone flashlight, keeping the beam aimed at the floor, just in case. Even if there was no one in here, the sight of a moving light in what was supposed to be an abandoned building could arouse the interest of anyone who happened to be passing.

Our boots echoed on the stone floors as we paced the building. There was no one around, not even any sign of a person.

"Fuck. What do we do now?" Saint voiced the question we'd all been thinking. I hated the hopelessness in his tone.

"There has to be something we missed." Turning on my own flashlight, I began sweeping it back across the church, from left to right, still keeping it low. As I moved, my gaze caught on a tall statue in the far corner.

My breath caught in my throat, and I jogged over to the statue, closely followed by Mateo and Saint. "Look at this." I aimed the light at the base of the statue. "See those grooves in the floor?"

"It moves." Mateo caught on instantly, already placing his palms on the stone figure. Saint and I joined him, and together, we pushed.

The statue moved far more easily than I'd anticipated, revealing an opening in the floor, with steps leading down.

"Fuck," Saint whispered, as I shone my light into the entrance to what was most likely a crypt of some sort.

Fuck, indeed.

I crouched down in front of the entrance.

"Everly?" My call echoed through the darkness.

From below, there was a soft, answering cry.

9
SAINT

Her voice—fuck.
"*Cal.*" Her voice had been so hoarse.

Without thinking, the three of us took off running through the dark. The air was colder down here but a bit more suffocating. There was no light, and I would have never thought the church had this place underground.

Callum and Mateo quickly pulled out their phones and utilized the flashlights on them. My eyes quickly began to scan all the areas they kept lighting.

There were tombstones everywhere. Some were in good condition, others had the stones cracked.

"Everly?" I yelled her name. The question thundered through this space, and now it made sense why.

"I'm here," her voice answered back, sounding a bit more confident and closer.

"There," Mateo said.

Both he and Cal had their lights flashed toward her in a second.

Everly was on the ground with her hands resting above her head. She closed her eyes to shield her face from the intrusion of the light. That made my blood boil, and I knew I wasn't the only one feeling this way.

As we got closer, I could see her hands had been tied to the statue of a man. It was a huge statue and next to it stood a crypt.

Fuck—she must've been fucking scared.

Immediately, I kneeled in front of her, cupping her face in my hands while Cal and Mat worked on untying the ropes from the statue.

"Everrrly," I whispered as I touched her cold face.

"S-s-aint?" she questioned.

"You're safe now, baby," I told her as I held her in my arms. As soon as I held on to her, I buried my face in her hair. It smelled like dirt, but her essence was still there, and it calmed me a bit.

"Fuck, baby," Cal hissed as her hands became free.

I looked up at him, and although he was being delicate with her, his eyes were fucking burning. Her wrists were red and chafed from where she'd tried like hell to escape. Parts of her skin had broken, and there was a little bleeding.

"I tried to escape, but when the candles went out, I couldn't see what I was doing," she whispered as she turned to face Callum.

"Who. Hit. You?" Mateo suddenly asked.

He flashed the light to her face, blinding both Everly and me with the light.

Everly whimpered as soon as Mateo touched her cheek.

My heart was beginning to beat erratically. I felt so fucking helpless at the moment. I knew it was irrational, but I didn't like holding on to our girl like this. She got taken from us—and they were going to fucking pay.

"Answer him," I demanded, because her silence was speaking volumes right now.

I was beginning to shake with fury, and I was sure my brothers knew that, and right now, we needed to stay calm for her sake.

Callum transferred Everly from my arms to his. He tenderly kissed the bruising on her cheek.

"Can you tell us what happened, mamas?" Mateo reached for her hand and gently squeezed it to reassure her.

"Yeah, but can we get out of here?" she asked, her tone tired and defeated.

I reached for Cal's phone. Mateo went ahead to light the way for Everly and Cal. While they did that, I hung back a bit. I wanted to do more. To not feel as useless as I did now. I needed to get it together because I could only think about running to her uncle's house and beating his ass. My scholarship, blowing cover, none of that mattered right now.

Flashing the light on the statue, I found an engraving. It said Charles Blackstone.

Motherfuckers.

Leaving her here alone and scared.

I kept flashing the light when I came across faint footprints. Then I remembered what Everly had told us about the time she had followed her uncle and the mayor here.

Those sons of bitches. I ran out after them. We needed to keep an eye on this place and get a better look, but Everly's safety was the most important thing right now.

Once I came outside, they were already in old Glenda.

Callum was at the wheel with Everly laying on Mateo's lap. They noticed my spooked face but didn't comment on it. We were all on the same page. Tonight had been one long fucking night, and we all wanted it to end already.

At least the rain had stopped.

I climbed into the car, and Everly reached her hands toward mine.

"Let's go home, baby," I told her.

When we pulled into the house, she was fast asleep. None of us dared wake her, so we just laid her on the bed, making sure she was comfortable.

Once she was safe, we did a perimeter check of the compound. Now we were in the garage with one light on.

"We can't let her go back to her dorm," Callum said.

"Her uncle is the dean, so keeping her away from him will be tricky," Mateo added.

"She stays with us," Cal spoke the words we all had been thinking since the ride here.

"One of us stays with her at all times," I said.

Mateo chuckled. "She's not going to like that."

"As long as it keeps her safe," Callum agreed.

"Now, you wanna tell us why you looked spooked?" Mateo raised a brow.

We were kids when we vowed to get revenge for Erick, and at first, we were too young to be able to do anything, but it was the drive we needed to keep going. That bit of hope to hang on to. And now that dream was closer than ever, and it tasted like hell. But there was no backing out now.

"Remember what Everly said about something moving when she was there?"

"They keep them there?" Callum added right away.

"I saw an old set of prints that still went deeper, and if I'm not mistaken, there has to be another exit to that fucking crypt."

We all knew how massive this news was. We now had the players and the location. All we needed now was to wait until they fucked themselves over.

Callum's face was stoic, his mind probably going one thousand miles per hour before he began to speak.

"It's the perfect place to store their merchandise. No one

has access to those blueprints, thanks to the mayor. I bet the police department probably does routine checks occasionally to keep it from being completely vandalized. Not enough to arouse suspicion that it's being watched, but just enough to make it inconspicuous to them."

"They really had it all planned out, didn't they?" It was a rhetorical question.

We stood there, quiet, all of us tired, but like hell if we could get some sleep now.

"The car is almost finished," Mateo said.

Without another word, we all got to work. The least we could do was cheer up our girl the best we could once she woke up.

10

EVERLY

When I woke, it took me a minute to get my bearings, before relief crashed over me. I was lying on soft sheets on Saint's bed, and I was *safe*.

The events of the past twenty-four hours caught up with me, and my whole body began to shake as tears filled my eyes. I needed comfort. I needed my three guys.

On trembling legs, I climbed off the bed and made my way through the house, but there was no sign of any of them. Through the open kitchen window, I could hear faint music coming from outside, so I let myself out of the house and made my way to the garage workshop.

Through the open door, I caught sight of Callum, and a smile spread across my face. I took a step forward, and he spun around and saw me.

"Baby." He came toward me, and I was suddenly wrapped up in his arms, resting my head against his chest as he stroked through my hair, pressing kisses to the top of my head.

Pulling back a little, he gripped my chin, tilting my head up to meet his eyes. "How are you feeling?"

"I'm okay." I was surprised to find that I meant it. I'd been through a nightmarish ordeal, but now I was here, I felt like I could take on anything with the Boneyard Kings at my side.

"Good. We'll talk about it later, okay? Come here," he murmured, lowering his head, and then his lips were on mine. I wound my arms around his neck as I opened up for him, losing myself in his kiss.

A throat clearing loudly next to us had us breaking apart, and I turned to see Saint, dressed in oil-smeared overalls, with a wide grin on his face. Callum released me, and Saint tugged me into him, kissing me with an intensity that made me breathless. "We were so worried about you." His lips trailed across my skin, down my jaw and onto my throat. "We're not letting you out of our sight again."

That was something we were going to have to discuss, but for now at least, there was nothing I wanted more than to be with them, away from rest of the world.

"Where's Mateo?" I glanced toward the open workshop, but Saint shook his head, exchanging a glance with Callum.

"He'll be out in a few." Running his hand down my arm, he slid his fingers through mine. "Wanna come and play with the crusher?"

Callum disappeared back inside the workshop, and I let Saint lead me over to where the big crusher machine was located, next to the small crane with a giant claw on the end of its arm.

"We use the crane to lift the cars once we've stripped them of everything useful, and dump them in the crusher." He moved toward the large metal crusher. "Cover your ears, this is gonna be loud."

I placed my hands over my ears, and he started up the crusher. Once it was running, he came back over to me, and climbed into the crane and held out his hand. When I was inside the small space, he reached around me to close the door, and pulled me onto his lap, my back to his chest.

"Mmm. Sitting here is more fun than it normally is." He placed one large hand on my thigh, and started kissing my neck, making me shiver. "Can you turn this on for us?"

As he said the words, he slid his hand higher. I angled my head around, kissing him back, and felt him smile against my lips.

"Is this a challenge?" I wriggled on him, and it was my turn to smile when he unsuccessfully tried to stifle a groan. I could feel him hardening beneath my ass, and I rocked back lightly. "Let's do this."

Switching on the crane engine, I waited for further instructions, tilting my head so he had better access to my throat.

His voice vibrated across my skin as his free hand covered mine, placing it on top of the lever to our right. "Use that lever to lift the arm of the crane. You see the blue car there? We're going to move the arm so that we can pick up the car and drop it into the top of the crusher."

Together, we moved the lever so the claw was in position over the car, and at the same time, Saint proved just how good he was at multitasking by sliding his hand all the way up my thigh, over my stomach, and then onto my breast.

"Saint." I arched back against him, the claw swinging as my hand slipped. He chuckled against me, correcting the claw's position, his fingers rubbing over my nipple and sending waves of pleasure through my body.

"Yeah?" His voice was so innocent.

"You know what." Grinding down on his hardness, I was rewarded with another groan.

"Everrrrly. Stop that. Concentrate on the crane." He

rolled my nipple between his fingers, and I gasped. "We need to get the claw to pick up the car. Hold it steady while I just..." Reaching to the side, he did something with the control panel which I couldn't focus on, now that he was stroking over my other breast while he licked and sucked the skin of my neck. The claw closed over the car, catching on the underside of the roof, and then he closed his fingers around my hand and together, we used the lever to lift the car into the air.

His hand left my breasts, sliding back down, over my stomach, and lower still. Because there were arms on either side of the seat restricting our movement, he pushed one finger down between my legs, putting pressure on my clit over my clothes. I moaned. It wasn't enough. I needed more.

"Later, I'm going to do everything to you. All three of us are. We need it, and you need it, don't you?"

"Yes. *Yes*. So badly." I needed them more than I'd ever needed anything before.

"We'll take care of you."

The crane arm was now in position over the top of the crusher, and he lifted his hand from between my legs and hit something on the control panel to open the claw, dropping the car into the crusher.

There was a loud scraping noise as the machine's rotating metal teeth began to effortlessly chew the car into pieces, and I watched, fascinated, temporarily distracted from the gorgeous guy holding me. He didn't let me forget him for long, though, tugging my earlobe with his teeth and biting down.

Another moan fell from my throat. "Saint. I wish we had more room."

His grip on me loosened. Turning off the crane, he sighed.

"So do I, but we have to wait until after your surprise. I'm so fucking hard right now, and now I have to go back out there with a boner, and Matty's gonna give me shit."

I laughed, but then his words registered, and I twisted to look at him. "Surprise? What surprise?"

He gave me a wide grin, excitement sparkling in his green eyes. "You'll see."

11

MATEO

"I do not owe you twenty dollars." Saint trailed after me.

Callum laughed.

"Bro, you fucking lost," I spoke over my shoulder as I put away the bucket of water.

Everly had hopped in the shower. She seemed to be handling everything like a fucking champ. We were so fucking proud of her.

"I didn't lose," Saint grumbled as we finished polishing the car.

"We said you wouldn't go five minutes without getting hard. You didn't even make it past two."

He said nothing, and we knew we had guessed right. Not like any of us would have done any better.

"If you're broke, Matty, just say that."

I flipped Saint off.

Today we all felt lighter. Not like we got much sleep, but at least we had Lorenzo off our backs. The mayor was a complication but had nothing to do with what happened with Everly.

Most importantly, Everly was now safe and in our care.

And the last thing, we finally had one of our biggest breakthroughs.

"You know there's a fifty percent chance she'll be furious we lied to her," I told them. With Everly, you didn't know which way she would go.

"Angry sex is the best sex," Saint added.

The three of us leaned on the hood of her car. We were waiting for the moment she came looking for us.

I wasn't the only one who needed her. There was nothing like making your woman scream for you to make sure that she was fine and no one's arms would harm her.

We heard the dingy door screech, and the three of us straightened our backs. We were close to losing it.

"What's going on?" Everly questioned as she came toward us.

Her hair was still wet from her shower. The shirt she'd borrowed fell to her thighs. I bit my lip to remind myself that first, her gift, then we could have fun after.

"Come here, mamas." I crooked my index finger toward her, my voice coming out deeper than I had intended.

Her eyes went molten. She looked at the three of us, and her pale cheeks got a lovely tint to them.

Oh yeah, she was itching for it too.

"I wouldn't count getting laid as a surprise," she sassed once she was standing in front of us.

None of us made a move to grab her, not yet. We blocked her view so we could see her full reaction.

The moment Cal and Saint began to move out of the way, I did the same. Our attention was solely on Everly.

Her eyes went wide, and that pouty mouth opened in shock.

"I don't understand," she managed to say.

She walked closer until she was standing in front of the

car. Her eyes gleamed with unshed tears. She tentatively brought her hands down to the hood. When they began to tremble, that was when we lost our restraint.

Saint's horny ass went behind her, wrapped his arms around her waist, and rested his head on her shoulder. Callum and I stuck to her sides. Callum stroked her cheek while I lightly pinched her hip.

"How?" She looked at all of us, then back at the car.

The car she loved so much, the only thing she had of her dad's, was now restored to its original condition. It was a true classic now. The wheels were brand spanking new, and we'd polished the shit out of it. The car fucking sparkled, and the interior was all redone. The only thing we'd preserved was the stereo.

"You think we were going to throw away the one thing you had of your dad's?" Saint asked, then kissed her cheek.

"But you said..."

Callum pulled Everly toward him. He cupped her face in his hands.

"Baby, we lied," he rasped against her lips.

"We knew you loved that piece-of-shit car," I said as I pulled her toward me. "So we made it something worthy of you."

I let myself have just a small taste of her lips as well. When I let her go, she went to inspect the car. Her hands were touching every single detail, marveling at all the work we had done. Getting everything had been a bitch, especially keeping it a secret from her— but damn if it wasn't worth it.

At first, we told ourselves that it was the least we could have done after her accident. It was a way to atone for the mistake we made. Then as time went on, we did it because we wanted to see her happy. And there was something about watching your girl ride in something you built from scratch.

"It's so beautiful," she mused. She then chewed her lip and looked at the three of us with those doe eyes, and my cock hardened, and if I had to guess, Cal was in the same boat. Saint had zero self-control. "I'll pay for it. It's too much."

"Like hell you will," Cal was the first to reply.

"We did this because you're our girl." Saint winked at her.

"The amount of work this must've taken," she still argued as her fingers trailed over the restored seats.

"Worth every second," Cal said in a husky tone. "The way you're looking at us now—*fuck*."

"I suggest you run to the house, mamas, unless you want to get fucked right here," I spoke.

The air went electric, filled with lust.

"We get our dicks in you, baby, and we are not stopping," Saint groaned.

Everly looked at us, and a wicked smile crossed her face before she took off running into the house.

12

CALLUM

"Listen up," I told Mateo and Saint as we followed Everly into the house at a leisurely pace, letting her get a head start. "We take it easy with her today. We still need to talk about what she went through, and if we go hard like I know we all want to, she's not going to be in a fit state to talk after."

"Yeah, baby, let's make sweet, sweet lurve." Saint thrust his hips obscenely and I rolled my eyes at his antics, while Mateo snorted.

"As long as we're all on the same page." I shut and locked the door behind us, then followed my brothers through the house to Saint's bedroom.

We all stopped dead in the doorway, and I sucked in a breath, my dick going from half hard to a fucking steel pipe in seconds.

Fuck. Me. Everly was there, lying on the white bedsheets, completely naked, with her legs open and her finger circling her clit. Her hair spilled out all over the pillows, a sign of how hurriedly she'd taken off her clothes, and as we stared at her, she bit down on her pouty bottom lip, watching us from beneath her lowered lashes.

She was so fucking beautiful, and so fucking ours.

As I took a step closer, I noticed the marks marring her creamy skin. Red marks on her wrists, bruises dotting her body, and on her arms, the telltale imprint of bruising in the shape of fingers.

Rage swept through my body, and I knew that the three of us would destroy the world for her.

"New plan. Fucking is off the table," I murmured quietly to Saint and Mateo. They both nodded, seeing what I was seeing. There was no doubt that our girl was strong, but she was delicate at the same time, and right now, she needed us to take care of her, whether she knew it or not.

"Look at you, baby," I rasped, moving to the foot of the bed. My gaze swept down her body, then back up again as I palmed my cock through my pants, and I noticed with satisfaction how her pupils dilated and her cheeks flushed. "So wet for us already. You want to come?"

She nodded, and I crawled up onto the bed as Mateo and Saint came to stand on either side of me.

Starting at her foot, I began to trail my fingers up her leg. "Use your words, Everly."

"Yes." Her sigh turned into a moan as Saint dipped his head to her breast, sucking her nipple into his mouth, while Mateo pressed his lips to her throat.

I lowered my head to her leg, kissing up her calf slowly, the three of us teasing her with light touches that would soak her pussy and drive her crazy, until she was begging for us. My cock was so fucking hard, straining against the confines of my pants as I kissed her soft skin, and I had to pause for a second to adjust myself.

"Why don't you take off your clothes?"

I glanced up to see Everly eyeing me with a suggestive smile curving over her lips, and it made me even harder. Wasting no time, I started tugging off my clothes, and when her gaze turned to Mateo, then Saint, they followed suit.

She moaned, her finger working harder over her clit. Her pussy was glistening with her arousal, and I just wanted my cock inside her, or failing that, to use my mouth and my fingers to make her come.

Saint took his hand off his dick long enough to curve his fingers over hers, pulling her hand away. He gave a wicked grin at her whine of protest. "Not yet." Then he placed her hand on his dick, and threw his head back with a groan as she curved her fingers around his erection.

She reached out for Mateo with her other hand, and proved just how good she was at multitasking when she started jerking him, her thumb stroking over the head of his cock, and my own cock jumped as I watched the way she was pleasuring them.

Her eyes met mine again, and she licked her lips. "Come up here."

I wanted to fuck her mouth so badly, but at the same time, I was trying to hang on to the shreds of my self-control, reminding myself that we were supposed to be taking it easy. She looked so tempting, though, spread out in front of me, making my brothers slowly lose control as she used her talented hands to bring them to the edge.

"Not yet, baby." Crawling over her body, I lowered myself over her, letting my hard length slide over her soaked pussy, grinding down into her so that she got friction all over her most sensitive areas. She gasped, arching into me, and I dragged my thick cock over her clit, then back down across her pussy. It would have taken no effort just to angle my hips and slide right inside her, but I resisted, even though it took everything I had. I'd never known anyone like Everly before. Someone who could make me lose control so easily, who owned every fucking part of me, just as she did with my brothers. She was our missing piece and...

A thought hit me so hard it made my head spin.

I think I love her.

Fuck.

If I was thinking it, Mateo and Saint wouldn't be too far behind, if they weren't already there.

Everly Walker had somehow become everything to us.

We'd die for her.

I slammed my mouth down on hers, needing to taste her, and she responded instantly, her legs coming around me to hold me in place as my tongue slid against hers. I felt Mateo and Saint both drop a hand to my shoulders, which might've been weird in the past, but now felt completely right in this moment. We were all in this together, and our goal was to make our girl forget about all the shit she'd been through, and feel pleasure like she'd never felt before.

"We're gonna make you come so fucking hard," I growled against her lips, nipping at the tender skin and feeling her shudder beneath me.

She blinked, slow and heavy-lidded, and gave me one of those sexy smiles that went straight to my cock. "You are? In that case, maybe you'd better get your dicks inside me. Now."

13

SAINT

The moment I saw Everly run away, my dick begged for a release. Those plans had changed when I saw her lying naked on the bed. Sure, she was a fucking goddess, and I wanted to fuck her until her pussy was leaking from all the cum she was getting from my brothers and me. But those marks, they fucking infuriated us.

Something as lovely and delicate as our girl shouldn't have been tainted by the cruelty of this world.

Those plans of delicacy went out the window the moment our little Everly began to beg for it.

I could see how Callum's control started to slip off, which turned me on even more. Add the fact that Everly had her hand wrapped around my throbbing cock, and I was ready to lose it.

One quick look at the other side, and I could see Mateo was feeling the same way. His eyes were on Everly with an intensity that was new.

Something had shifted in all of us. She was more than just our girl. She was a taste of hope, and for guys like us that had been starving, we were ready to take it all.

I wouldn't call this lust—it was so much more.

Cal's dick glided between Everly's folds, and I knew how good it felt to have that wetness coating your dick. Callum bent to kiss her, and Mateo and I used his body for support.

"We're gonna make you come so fucking hard," Cal groaned.

Everly's hand tightened around me and moved faster against Mateo.

"You are? In that case, maybe you'd better get your dicks inside me. Now."

Fuck, the way she sounded so needy, I knew none of us would be able to resist.

Her hips started to move, and I knew she was grinding her needy pussy against Callum. Her eyes fluttered, and moans began to fall from her lips.

"You look so fucking hot," Mateo hissed.

Everly moaned louder.

"Give her what she wants, Cal," Mateo commanded.

"Yes," Everly breathed.

"Fuck her greedy little cunt."

Everly opened her legs wider, and Cal was transfixed, looking down at her. His hips moved back, denying her what she wanted most, then he slowly entered her. It was so fucking hot watching the way Everly's eyes fluttered as Cal filled her up, and how Cal reacted to her wet heat.

"Baby, I need your mouth," I begged.

"Yes," she moaned in agreement.

Mateo turned her face toward me. He removed her hand from his dick and instead bent to whisper in her ear.

"Fuck, she just got wetter," Cal hissed.

"Show Saint what that mouth can do," he then instructed.

Hell yeah. Everly opened her mouth and looked at me

through half-mast eyes. Slowly, my dick slid inside of her, and every time Cal thrust into her, she would take me deeper.

"*Shit,*" I cursed when she deep-throated me.

I closed my eyes for a second, and then Everly was sucking me harder, and her moans around my dick came faster. Mateo was sucking on her tits. He alternated between licking her pink nipples and lightly biting them.

"You want our cum, baby?" Mateo groaned as he kissed her navel.

"Cal," she moaned around my dick in answer. "Please."

For someone who wanted to take it slow today, he sure as fuck lost it when she begged him. One of his hands went to her clit and began to play with it as his hips moved faster.

Everly started to orgasm. Her gaze was locked on mine as she moaned around my dick. I was about to lose it.

"Don't come in her mouth, do it on her tits," Mateo hissed. He was jerking himself off, his mouth alternating between her jawline and neck.

I pulled out of Everly's mouth, and she turned her head and began to kiss Matty. My hand moved faster as I watched the way she let us own her completely.

My cum covered her chest and tits, down to her belly button.

"Watch out," Cal warned right before he flipped her.

He fixed her hips and began to pound into her. The sounds that his skin made against her ass was fucking hot.

Everly opened her mouth to moan, but Matty was sliding his cock inside her before a sound could come out.

"Is this what you wanted, mamas?" he groaned as he pulled her hair into a tight fist. "For us to fucking own you?"

My dick was hard again as I watched them overload her senses. Her mouth was filled with Mateo's dick when her eyes landed on me, and she stretched her hand for me to use.

"Fuck," Callum hissed.

When he pulled out, part of his cum landed on Everly's lower back.

Mateo pulled her away.

"Pass me the lube." He nodded toward me.

"She's so fucking wet, I don't think she'll need it," Cal rasped.

Going to my nightstand, I threw the lube on the bed.

Mateo came to the edge of the bed as Cal helped Everly up. He kissed her as he guided her to Mateo's lap. She was facing me, and I winked at her.

Cal sat next to them and began to kiss her again. It was fine. Those weren't the lips I wanted. I kneeled at their feet and spread her legs. Cal instantly grabbed one, helping me keep her open.

She squirmed when I kissed her inner thigh. Mateo used that opportunity to insert one finger inside of her.

"Oh fuck," she whimpered when Matty began to finger-fuck her ass.

I smiled against the apex of her thighs. One of her hands came to my hair and ran her fingers through it. My tongue peeked out, and I grazed it against the entrance of her pussy, slowly pushing the tip inside of her.

She was drenched.

Having a taste of her, I couldn't keep teasing her. I wanted to lap her all up. I began to fuck her with my tongue. Her hips moved against me.

"She's ready for your dick," I told Mateo.

14

EVERLY

My senses were on overload. The three of them had their hands and mouths all over me, and everything was hot and wet and so, so good. My jaw ached from sucking Mateo and Saint, and I'd only just come, but I could feel it rising up inside me again. The three of them knew how to play my body in a way that I'd never known before, and I knew that I'd never get enough of them.

Mateo eased his fingers out of my ass and placed his hands around my waist. Saint's tongue drew back, and I immediately missed it, but then Mateo and Callum were lifting me, lining me up with Mateo's dick. I breathed out a long, shuddering breath when the head of his cock entered my ass. Sinking down on him, I moaned, throwing my head back against his shoulder. Fuck. I was so full.

Saint replaced his tongue with his fingers, thrusting two of them inside of me, then three, timing them with Mateo's rhythm as he began pounding in and out of me. Callum's hands were on my body, touching me everywhere, driving me wild at the same time. It was too much, and not enough, all at the same time. The three of them consumed me, and it felt like only seconds before I was shuddering against them, coming all over Saint's fingers. He groaned, long and low, withdrawing his fingers from me and spreading my wetness over his cock.

"Fuck, that's so fucking hot," Callum rasped, fisting his own cock as he moved closer to me. His hand moved faster as Mateo gripped me more tightly, burying his head in the crook of my neck.

"Your ass feels so good," he groaned, thrusting up hard. I could feel his dick throbbing as he came inside me, and the sensation was so good that I couldn't help crying out, twisting my head to give him a messy, breathless kiss. The next moment, Saint and Callum's cum was hitting my body, and then I was encircled by the three of them, completely wrung out, completely satiated, and completely theirs.

Safe, with the three guys that had become my entire world.

When we were all recovered and cleaned up, I knew it was time to discuss what had happened. We all seemed to be prolonging having the conversation, not wanting to shatter the moment. Saint took the longest time ever to make me a hot chocolate while Mateo and Callum tucked me under a blanket, then decided that the one they'd used wasn't good enough, and it took another ten minutes for them to dig out another one which looked almost identical to the first.

But eventually, we couldn't put it off any longer. Callum slid his fingers through mine, and as I sipped my hot chocolate, Mateo and Saint stroked over my legs.

Mateo's brown eyes met mine, soft and full of compassion. "Are you gonna tell us what happened?"

I took a deep breath. "Yeah. The first thing you should know is, the police chief is the other guy that was there that night at the church."

There was total silence, and the three of them exchanged glances. I got the feeling that if they hadn't known it already, they'd had their suspicions. As I recounted the rest of my story and then they told me what had happened to them, it began to feel more and more like a nightmare. The mayor had been shot, and they'd been implicated? What the fuck was this Lorenzo's endgame?

We now knew who the three major players were, even if we weren't completely sure what they were up to. The three most powerful men in Blackstone, and there was no doubt in my mind that they would not let me escape this easily. I hadn't admitted to anything, so they didn't know for certain what I knew, but I wasn't about to underestimate them. They had to be smart, ruthless, and sneaky to get to where they were.

But I was counting on one fact. The sort of men they were used to dealing with—they were nothing like the Boneyard Kings. It only took one wrong move, and the game would go in our favor.

"Here's what we do," Callum spoke up at last. "We call in every favor. And I mean, *every* favor. I don't care what it takes, whose dicks you have to suck—we find out exactly what the fuck is going down, and how it connects to Erick and Dave. That happens now. We've been too complacent for too long, and now we're paying the price. "In the meantime, Everly, you do not leave here. For any reason. You'll be safe here, but none of us can guarantee your safety outside these walls."

I knew he spoke sense, but I still protested. "What about my things? My laptop? I don't think there's anything incriminating on it, but what if there is?"

Saint spoke up. "I'm going back to the frat house. We need to act normal for now. Give me your keys, and I can get one of the guys to sneak in. Half of those fuckers will do anything to get their hands on more coke, and they know we're good for it."

"Okay. I don't like this, but I think until we know more, going about our business as normal and keeping Everly out of sight is the best way to play it." Callum rubbed his thumb across my hand, then turned to Mateo. "Can you speak to Lorenzo? See if you can find out what his endgame is, and what he knows. After the shit he pulled with the mayor, I want assurances that we're not going to take the blame. He implicated us in his power games, but we all know he's loyal to the south side. Fuck, he's on a level with the mayor in their eyes. My gut says that he won't double-cross us, but I still don't trust him."

Mateo nodded. "It's done."

Callum leaned back against the headboard, blowing out a heavy breath. "I'll get in touch with all the contacts we have that could be useful, and chase up our guy who was doing the trace on those account numbers we found at the mayor's house. We need that information, now."

Mateo and Saint gave him a nod of agreement. Picking up my mug of hot chocolate, I took a sip, feeling the soothing warmth slide down my throat. "What am I supposed to do? We're a team, aren't we? I can't just sit around here doing nothing."

"Uh." Saint's eyes flicked to Callum's before returning to mine. "It might be time to go through the rest of the old man's things. See if there's anything else we missed." There was an uncomfortable silence, where Mateo bowed his head and Callum's fingers tightened around mine, but eventually, they both made noises of agreement.

We had the beginnings of a plan. I knew it wouldn't be enough, but it was a start.

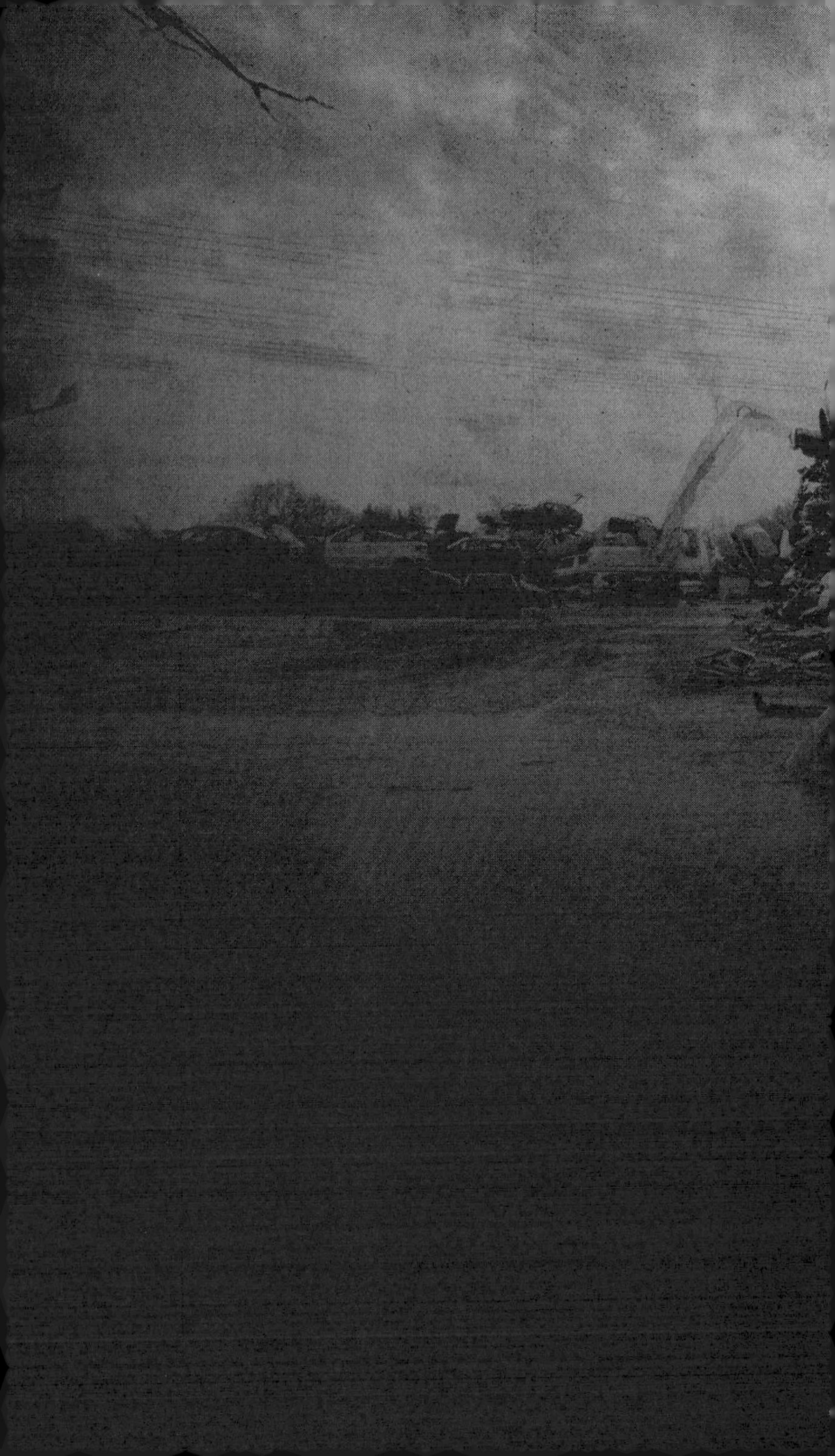

15

MATEO

We were still debating if knowing all the players in the game made it better or worse. It all made so much sense. The dean controlled the trade from within. The mayor kept the rumors away, and the fucking chief made sure there was no trail.

It was an unholy trinity if I ever saw one.

When Monday came, we were all anxious to go back to school. So far, we had someone keeping an eye on the church. We needed to know the ins and outs of it all, but we didn't want people to know about the catacombs, at least not yet.

"People are going to talk," Everly said before we got to school.

They would. At least Saint left for school yesterday, so this way, it wouldn't be the three of us with her. Not that we cared, but her uncle would.

I reached for Everly's hand. She was sitting in the middle of Callum and me.

"It's all good, mamas," I told her. "People talk out of envy."

She seemed content with that answer. Her hair was fixed so that the small bruising on her cheek didn't show. One thing I knew for sure was that her uncle would pay for that one. There was nothing I hated more than a man lifting his hand to a woman. He wasn't a man at all if he brought a woman to heel by force. He was a pussy.

"I'll wait outside," I told Everly.

Callum pulled her closer to him, and then he kissed her. I looked around, trying to see if her uncle was keeping a tab on us. If I were him, I would. The doors to the truck opened. Callum went the other way, while Everly and I made our way to her first class.

"Everyone is staring," Everly whispered.

Probably because I was never seen alone with a girl.

"Do you care?" I stopped and stared at her.

She bit her lip, and I loved when she did that. Drove me nuts. And now, all I could think about was how she looked taking our dicks.

She took a step forward and held on to my hand. I looked at it for a second. This was definitely fucking new. I'd never had a girl that I called mine.

"Let's get you to class, mamas." I smirked.

I got her to her class, and she began to walk in. I pulled her back by the waistband of her jeans.

"Didn't you forget something?" My voice was husky. I pushed her next to the wall. My hands were on either side of her.

"If you want something, then you should take it." She gave me a gloating smile.

I leaned down and licked her lower lip. I then pulled it into my mouth, sucking it. She let out a soft moan. My dick hardened. I gave her a sweet kiss, because anything more and I would lose control.

When I pulled away, I could see her want written all over that pale face.

"Ignore the rumors," I told her. "There was never a girl interesting enough to get a hold of Callum's attention. A girl that Saint wanted more than one night with." Her breath hitched. "A girl who made me want to fucking try. That's why I always let Saint lead. Because no girl was worth my effort."

I pinched her chin.

"Go to class, mamas. Cal will meet you after."

After dropping her off, I went to the other side of campus by the baseball fields. I needed somewhere semi-private to talk. And for some reason, by the bleachers, no one would care. Some would be doing drugs, others trying to fuck, so everyone minded their own business.

"Thanks for coming," I told Lorenzo.

He looked different than he usually did. More relaxed, and if I didn't know any better, I would think he was a student here. He was young, and power like his was probably inherited.

"*Compa*," he greeted.

"How's the mayor?" I asked.

He smiled.

"He's learning his place," he told me.

I knew what we needed to do, and Lorenzo didn't mess with the shit the dean, mayor, and chief did, so telling him the whole truth could be the only way to get him to play nice with us. Knowing Blackstone's ins and outs would make him king of everything once everyone was dealt with. And that was what we were counting on. For him to want to help us for his own gain.

"I have a deal for you," I said.

The smile he gave me was scary, and if I was a lesser

man, I would have pissed my pants.

"What is it?"

So I told him everything, hoping his intel could shine a light on all the shit we had missed.

"You want the mayor to be a rat, don't you? Let him go so he can report to us?"

Essentially, yeah, that was the plan we came up with. Those three were so deep in each other's shit they wouldn't trust anyone. So we needed to pit them against each other.

"We think that's the best way to get them."

He thought about it for a second.

"One condition," he said.

We knew this was coming, but we could no longer play it safe, not when Everly was on the line.

"Lo que sea." Whatever it is, I told him.

"Your hands better end up as bloody as mine."

I extended my hand to shake his.

I sighed in relief once he left. Classes would be ending soon, and Cal should be on his way to Everly. I called him first since I knew I'd see Saint next.

"What did he say?" Cal greeted.

"He wants insurance," I told him.

Yeah, he wasn't stupid. He wanted all of us to get our hands dirty because if something went wrong, the blame wouldn't be on him.

"Then we better play this game better than him," Cal said before he hung up.

And we would. We would have ticked off every box in our revenge list by the end. And if we were lucky, we would come out of this unscathed. Even if we weren't, we agreed nothing touched Everly.

"It took a long time, Erick, *pero por fin.*"

Finally.

16

EVERLY

My butterfly ring was missing.

Now that I thought about it, I remembered the clatter as it fell to the floor inside the catacombs. I swallowed the lump in my throat, rubbing across my bare finger. My stomach was already churning at the thought of what my uncle might do to me now that I was back on campus. And now this—I gained back the part of my dad that I'd thought I had lost forever, but now I'd lost the part of my mum that I kept with me always.

It had taken me a while to realize it was missing. With everything that had happened—being kidnapped, then rescued, then back with the Boneyard Kings, I hadn't had a chance to think about anything else, but now, my worries were overtaking me.

I took a deep breath, reminding myself that I was as safe as I could be. The Boneyard Kings wouldn't leave me alone —I had some of my classes with them, and for those I didn't, one of them would be there for me between classes, so I didn't have to walk anywhere alone.

Mia and Hallie slipped into the seats next to me, on the

back row. Hallie eyed me curiously. "Girl, where have you been? You haven't been answering any of my texts."

"Or mine," Mia interjected.

Guilt hit me on top of everything else. "I'm sorry. I've been..." *Locked up by my crazy uncle. Kidnapped by the chief of police. Had the best orgasms of my life in an orgy with three guys from the wrong side of the tracks. Fallen for said guys, despite the danger we were in.* "...busy with schoolwork," I finished lamely.

It was obvious neither of them bought my excuse, but thankfully, our professor started speaking, and they fell silent.

I attempted to take notes, but it was a lost cause, and I was almost grateful for the sudden disruption at the front of the room when there was a loud knock at the door, followed by one of the administrative staff stepping inside. There was a whispered conversation with our professor, and then he was speaking.

"Everly Walker. Miss Walker? Would you please come down here?"

Biting down on my lip, I shot a look at Mia and Hallie, who stared at me, wide-eyed. I slowly gathered up my things, attempting to calm my racing heart, and then made my way to the front, with all eyes on me.

"Miss Walker. Please come with me." The woman from the administrative office indicated toward the door, and I had no choice but to step outside. She led me through the corridors, and it didn't take long to work out where she was taking me. I'd been half expecting it anyway. My uncle wouldn't let me get away with being back on campus like nothing had happened.

When we reached the office with the shiny plaque which read "Dean Walker," I sucked in a sharp breath. The woman rapped on the door twice, and then turned the handle. "He's expecting you," she said, giving me a gentle nudge over the threshold.

Then the door closed behind me, and I was alone with my uncle.

Seated behind his huge desk, he eyed me over the top of his glasses. His expression gave nothing away, and I grew more and more apprehensive as the silence stretched, but I refused to let it show on my face.

He eventually broke the silence, stretching out a hand. "Take a seat, Everly."

I lowered myself into the chair across from his, using all my strength to keep my composure. I held his gaze, and I thought I could detect a small glimmer of respect in his eyes. There was no doubt in either of our minds anymore that we were opponents. The board had been set, and the first plays had been made. It was his move now.

"I believe that there has been a misunderstanding. A quite significant misunderstanding, in fact." Steepling his fingers under his chin, he watched me, like a cat might watch a mouse. Ready to pounce at any time.

"Oh?" I kept my voice light.

"Yes. Everly... I apologize." He sighed heavily. "My actions were... inexcusable."

What. The. Fuck? Only my fingernails digging into my palms kept me from launching out of my seat in shock. I knew my eyes had widened, and I quickly schooled my expression as best I could.

A cold smile curved over his lips, and it chilled me to the bone. "You have every right to be angry with me, Everly. Allow me to make it up to you in some small way." Standing, he came around the side of his desk to stand in front of me, and he extended his hand. My heart was beating out of my chest, but I unclenched my fingers and lifted my own hand.

Something cool and metallic dropped into my palm.

My butterfly ring.

This time, I couldn't stop the gasp that fell from my lips, and I blinked fast to push back the sudden tears that were threatening.

"A token of my goodwill. I found it, and I wanted to return it to you. I know how much it means to you."

He didn't have to say where he'd found it—we both knew where it had come from. A flashback of that oppressive, airless space came to me, trapped in the darkness with no way out, and bile rose up in my throat.

"Thank you," I managed to croak, closing my fingers around the precious object. I didn't want to speak those words to him; I wanted to shout, and rage, to ask him why he had done this, but I held my tongue.

He slightly inclined his head, before moving back around his desk to take a seat again. "I trust that there will be no more issues?"

"No."

"Good. You're free to leave."

I slid the ring onto my finger, the feel of it back in its rightful place calming me, then slowly rose to my feet, gripping the strap of my book bag. When I made it to the door, he called my name.

"Everly?"

Turning to meet his gaze, I took a deep breath. "Yes?"

His eyes grew hard, and his tone became low and threatening. "If you even *think* about stepping out of line... you'll regret it."

17

SAINT

It was my turn to pick up Everly from class, but she wasn't there after it ended. Naturally, I began to freak out. I'd just taken my phone from my pocket to ask one of my brothers if they had seen her, when it started to ring.

Tiff, the caller ID read.

For the first time in forever, I forgot about my fucked-up mother. With all the shit that had been going on, I forgot to call her back. At least she wasn't dead, right? There was some sort of fucked-up consolation in the fact that if she was calling to be a pain in the ass, it meant she was still breathing.

"Hello," I answered, wondering if I would get hysterics or a sob fest.

"Hello?" her scratchy voice screeched. "That's all you're going to say after ghosting me? I could have been dying in some ditch somewhere, for all you knew!"

I rolled my eyes.

"How much?" I said right away as I walked faster, trying to see if Everly was among the stream of students who had just been dismissed. This wouldn't be my life if the old man were still alive. Tiff would have stayed away after the deal she made with him. But as soon as she heard he died, she came crawling back.

I wondered why she listened to the old man. Yeah, Dave was scary, but he wouldn't have hurt her. She was my mom.

"A thousand dollars," she demanded in a greedy voice.

I stopped dead in my tracks and laughed.

"You realize I'm a broke college student, right?"

"Don't play dumb with me, Saint. I know you can get the cash."

"No, Tiffany, I really can't," I bit out. "Two hundred or nothing," I told her as I spotted Mia and Hallie, but no Everly with them.

"You don't know how hard it is to sur—"

Her hysterics were grating on my nerves. All she did was whine, beg, and abuse. She was nothing like Everly, who didn't ask for anything and gave us everything she could freely.

Then it hit me harder than a set of plastic double *D*'s smacking me in the face. I loved her. Fuck, I was in love with Everly.

"Then get a job, Tiff. Shit, start charging for all the fucking shit you do for free, but don't try to put that shit on me," I said, feeling like the chains she had around me was starting to get loose.

"I'm still your mama, you ungrateful brat," she spat before hanging up on me.

Good thing she did, or else I would have probably finished cutting the ties that loosely kept us together, and I wasn't sure how I felt about that. I knew it was fucked up, but having a toxic relationship with Tiff was all I'd learned, and I wasn't sure if I was ready for the detox.

Hallie and Mia spotted me right away. Hallie glared at

me while Mia gave me a small smile. I tried to keep my distance for Everly's sake since it was her choice on whom she let into her life, but I already knew girls like Hallie would never accept the type of relationship me and my brothers had with her. They would try to taint it out of jealousy and make it seem like she was our whore rather than see that we worshiped the ground she walked on.

"Hey." I grinned at them. "What happened to Everly? She was supposed to be with you?"

"Maybe she left with Callum or Mateo," Hallie bit out. She had every intention to cause trouble with that comment.

Mia looked down, and I didn't mind her. She was just one of those girls who wasn't very confrontational with her friends.

This was ridiculous. After Tiff, my patience was running a little bit thin.

Before I could say more, Everly's voice rang out, and I felt relief hit me.

"Sorry I'm late," she said in a breathy tone.

Two things happened when I heard that tone. My cock got hard, and I also knew she was rattled, and her skin wasn't that lovely shade because she was flushed.

Our eyes met, and she didn't have to say the words for me to know I had been right. We were at school, so the only thing that meant was her uncle had made a move.

"It's okay. You're right on time." I kept my tone light. "We were just heading to go to Peaches."

She seemed to understand we needed to discuss what happened. While she said goodbye to her friends, I texted Cal and Mateo to meet us at the diner.

The ride was fairly quiet. We both knew what we needed to discuss, but we would wait for the others. There was no use in repeating the same information.

As soon as we pulled up to the road that led back into the other side of town, Cal and Mateo were behind us in the truck.

My hand went to Everly's thigh. "You want to show them what this car can really do?" I challenged her.

She turned to me with a wicked grin. It fucking sucked that this whole time we had been thrown into some deep shit, because girls like Everly deserved to smile often.

The Camaro took off and it was the distraction we needed. When we made it to the parking lot, we were both a little less on edge.

"What took you so long?" I asked Cal and Mateo as they parked next to us.

Neither said anything, just gave me their middle fingers.

Assholes.

We took our seats in our usual spot. It didn't take long for Esther to come and take our orders.

"Ohhhh," Esther exclaimed. "Same girl? Twice?"

She handed Everly a menu.

"Blink three times, sweetheart, if you want me to help you."

We all laughed.

"Why you gotta be like that, Esther?" Mateo smiled at the old hag.

She ignored Mateo and stared down at Everly.

"Out of all of them, you picked Saint?" she exclaimed as she pointed at me. I see where she would think that since Everly was sitting next to me.

Everly's cheeks went red.

"What if she's my girlfriend?" Callum threw out, and Everly's eyes flashed, and she bit her lip.

Esther looked at me and then at Cal, and finally at Mateo.

"Why not my Latin spice? You ain't racist, are you?" She raised a brow at Everly. It was cute to watch her work her way out of this one.

"She's most definitely not racist," Mateo winked.

There was a pause as Esther connected the dots.

"Ohhhh, child," she screeched as she clapped her hands, causing a few people to look our way. "You are proof that people can have heaven on earth. I mean, Saint is cute, but he's a little loudmouth, so you have two others to shut his ass up."

I gaped at her.

"Here, I thought you loved me." I brought my hands to my chest. "I tried to tell the guys you were the one for a long time, but they didn't listen.

Everyone was laughing.

Esther rolled her eyes.

"You're lucky I'm not younger, honey," she told Everly. "Back in my day, it would take these three and their daddy to keep a woman like me satisfied."

The three of us groaned.

"I need to scrub that image out of my mind." Mateo shook his head.

"Why were you picturing it in the first place, Matty?"

Everly turned to me. "So I was your second choice, after Esther?"

My brothers laughed.

I threw an arm around Everly. "You were the only choice, baby."

Esther brought our food and drinks. Before turning

away, she looked Everly dead in the eyes. "I ain't squeamish, honey. These three idiots step out of line, you tell your aunty Esther, and we will chop their dicks off."

Everly looked at us and smiled at Esther. "I think I can handle them."

After Esther left us alone, we talked about what happened today—well, everything except Tiff.

"He's planning something," Cal said after a while.

"That was a power play," Mateo agreed.

Dean Walker thought he had an ace up his sleeve, but so did we.

18

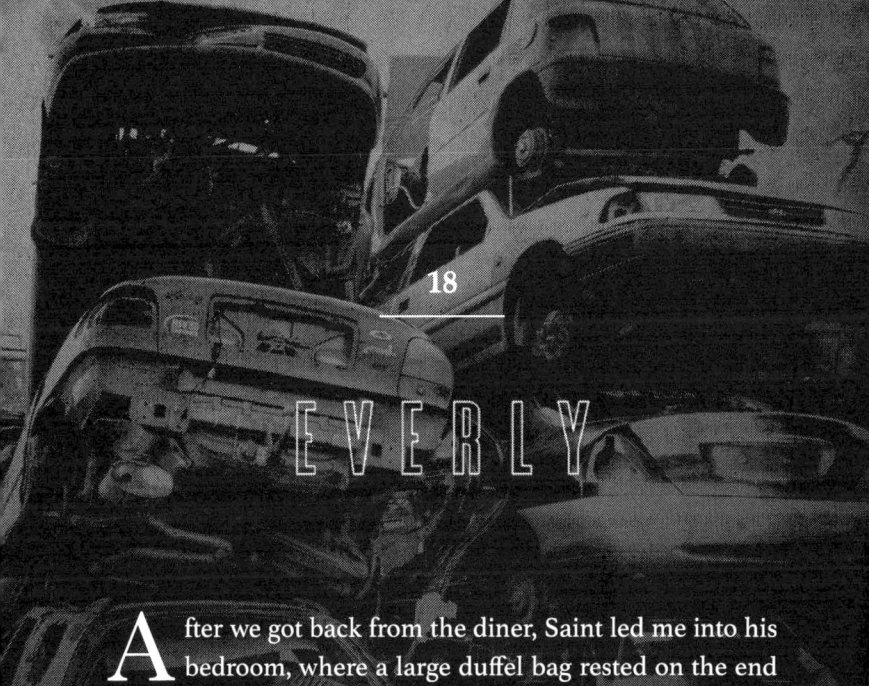

EVERLY

After we got back from the diner, Saint led me into his bedroom, where a large duffel bag rested on the end of his bed.

"Here. I got this for you."

I raised a brow, but made my way to the bed, and unzipped the bag. As soon as I laid eyes on the contents, a huge smile spread across my face.

My laptop, my framed photo of my parents, my makeup bag, books, clothes... in short, everything I needed from my room was there.

"Saint. Thank you." Crossing over to him, I threaded my arms around his waist. He wrapped his arms around me, kissing the top of my head.

"It was nothing. I bribed some of the frat guys to get everything you needed from your room."

"Still, thank you. This is everything I need."

He reached into the bag, lifting the photo. "Can I?"

I nodded, unsure of what he was doing, but I followed him out of his room, all the way through the house, until he stopped in the living room, in front of the mantelpiece

Carefully, he adjusted the framed photos on the mantelpiece until there was a space, and then he placed the picture of my parents next to them. "Good?"

There was a lump in my throat. "Good," I whispered, throwing my arms around him again. The next minute, I felt more bodies next to me, and I was surrounded by him, Callum, and Mateo.

When we broke apart, Callum tugged me to him, his hand gripping my chin and tilting my head back so I could look into his eyes. "Did you mean what you said about wanting to help out?"

"Yes." My reply was immediate.

He dipped his head to brush a kiss across my lips, then straightened up. "Okay. We have the old man's things to go through, if you want to look at them. Point out anything that looks like it could have something to do with Erick or the shit we're investigating."

"I can do that. Show me where."

He led me into what had clearly been Dave's room. There was a bed, a small wardrobe, and a desk with papers scattered haphazardly across it. I could hear Callum exhale a shaky breath as he crossed the threshold, and I blindly reached for his hand, slipping my palm into his and squeezing, in an attempt to give him some comfort. He smiled down at me, stopping in front of the desk. Shifting on his feet, his gaze grew distant. "Do you want to hear about the first time I came in here?"

My fingers tightened around his. "Tell me."

"Okay."

I was exploring the house. Mateo and Saint were outside—I could hear their voices through the open kitchen window. Their excitement was clear, and it made me happy. Finally, something was going our way. They'd both said it—we had a home now, and no one could take that away from us.

Something inside me still found it too good to be true, no matter what they said. I didn't trust easily. None of us did, but I guess out of the three of us, I was the most cynical.

Exiting the kitchen, I moved through the house, bypassing the rooms we'd already seen, and ended up in front of a closed door. I turned the handle, and it opened with a soft creak.

The room inside was plain. An unmade bed, a small wardrobe with the door slightly ajar, and a desk. Over the desk hung an enlarged photo in a wooden frame, slightly blurry, of the old man with a small boy.

I moved closer, raising my hand to the image.

Erick.

I missed him so much.

We all did.

"What are you doing here?"

I spun around at the noise, my heart pounding. Meeting the old man's gaze, I gritted my teeth and prepared myself for a verbal, or more likely a physical, lashing. I'd been trespassing. What was I thinking?

"Don't look at me that way, boy. I ain't gonna hurt you." The old man approached me slowly, his hands raised, palms to me, showing he was no threat. I eyed him with suspicion as he drew closer, my legs tensed, ready to bolt at any second.

His face crinkled, the lines becoming more pronounced as his brows pulled together. "I can't say I know how it's been for you boys in the past, but the three of you are safe here. My house is yours. Nowhere's off-limits. You're free to go wherever you want."

. . .

When Callum raised his head, his eyes were glassy, and the only thing I could do was hug him tightly, hoping that it would convey everything I couldn't put into words.

"I can take it from here," I said softly, sensing his need to escape. He gave me a grateful smile, dropping a quick kiss on the tip of my nose, before he disappeared and left me alone.

Giving a quick look around the room, I decided to make a start on the desk. It was the most obvious place, after all, and it looked like the guys had already started going through it. Taking out my phone, I pulled up my music app. When the low, sultry croon of Lana Del Ray filtered from the speakers, I took a seat on the floor, cross-legged, and began to go through the papers. I stacked them in piles—papers that weren't relevant, and papers that had potential.

After a while, when I had one teetering stack of irrelevant papers—mostly to do with cars that had come through the junkyard—and one small pile of potentials, I climbed to my feet to stretch out the kinks in my body. It felt like I'd been sitting here for hours. I glanced at my phone. I *had* been sitting here for hours.

Opening the top drawer of the desk, I lifted out the files that were inside, placing them on the desktop, and then went to open the second drawer. It wouldn't budge, so I yanked at it. It moved a little, but still refused to open, so I braced myself, and pulled as hard as I could. The drawer suddenly flew open, sending me careening backward, losing my balance and tumbling to the floor. There was a loud crash as the files I'd stacked on the top of the desk fell down, knocking off a pot of pens and a stapler in the process.

"Shit," I said aloud, climbing to my feet and gathering up the fallen items. Some of the files had disappeared down the back of the desk, and there was no way I could reach them without moving it.

Once I'd cleared a space, I carefully dragged the desk a couple of inches or so away from the wall, just enough that I could reach down the back. My fingers closed around the fallen files, and I gradually rescued them all, then moved the desk back into place.

I turned away to continue going through the papers, but something caught my eye. Spinning back around, I looked at the files I'd recovered.

There, at the top of the stack, was a folder that was different to the others. A soft, faded gray rather than the browns and yellows of the others.

I reached for it, flipping it open.

My eyes widened, and my fingers trembled as I scanned the contents.

Then, I grabbed the folder, and ran for the Boneyard Kings.

19

MATEO

The yard was huge, bigger than people probably thought. It wasn't until you looked at it with a sky view that you saw how much it covered.

Some of our contacts had reported more cop activity lately in the area, which only meant that the pressure to do so came from above. The chief and the dean were getting antsy.

What happened to the mayor was very hushed. The people were told he had an accident while playing golf; that was why he had been MIA. As for the dean and the chief, I knew they knew the real story, or as much as the mayor was allowed to say. For all his flaws, he didn't want his family hurt—at least not yet. I was sure it all led back to his image.

I was at the back, watching through the holes in the fence as a squad car drove by slowly. I wouldn't put it past them to trespass and try to pin something on us.

The cop parked the car, and it took a few seconds for the crunching of his boots to come closer. I smiled. Informants and information were only good if they were reliable. Something these dirty assholes were about to learn the hard way.

I waited for him to get closer and when he was close enough to hear but not be able to see much inside, I began to talk.

"No, next week," I said in a rushed-out voice. The cop came to a stop. "Yeah, by the old warehouse on the outskirts... Yeah, at midnight... I'll see you there..."

I pretended to walk away and watched as the cop got back in his car and drove away.

I smiled to myself.

Desperate people believed all kinds of lies. This had only been possible with the help of our community who'd been keeping us alerted, and we loved them for it.

Making my way back toward the house, I ensured that all the new cameras were working. It was an investment we couldn't afford, but it had to be done. If it meant we had to bust our asses even more, so be it. Everly's safety wasn't something we played with. After I'd checked the cameras, I made my way through the maze, and cleaned Lorenzo's last car. We hoped that he'd pick it up soon because it would be a weight off our shoulders.

When I came back, Saint and Callum were working on a car in the garage.

"Did he show up?" Cal asked.

"Yeah, he stayed there for a few then left," I told them.

"So now we wait..." Saint added.

We shook our heads.

Saint looked a bit uncomfortable, and both Cal and I knew why. We were just waiting for him to be the one to bring up the Tiffany subject.

He was a better man than us in that sense. Cal and I would have told that bitch to fuck off a long time ago.

"She needs money, doesn't she?" Cal asked.

"Yeah," Saint said without looking at us. "I know we need to pay for the cameras, so I'll work double."

"With school and practices on top of that?" I bit out. Not angry at him, but at what Tiff put him through.

Both Cal and I looked at one another, and then we pulled our wallets out, handing him a hundred each.

Saint shook his head. "I can't take that."

"You can and you will," I told him.

"We're able to save up, not a lot but some, since we don't have anyone hitting us up for cash," Callum added almost apologetically.

Saint was getting red, probably from anger.

"You'd do the same for us, so let us do this for you."

We stretched out our hands, trying to get him to take the money.

"Come on, man, it's not like we're asking you to suck our dicks in exchange," I joked, and Cal snorted.

Saint tentatively reached for the money. "You better not coerce me into sexual favors. I'll sue your asses for sexual harassment."

We laughed it off as he put the money in his pocket. Then the door to the garage opened. I turned around as Everly ran inside, holding on to one of the folders from the old man's bedroom.

"I found something," she rushed out breathlessly, probably from running.

Since I was the closest to her, I pulled her into my arms. I caressed her arms with my hands, and I could feel the goosebumps.

"Breathe," I whispered.

She nodded as she took a deep breath.

Callum came to stand in front of her. He took the folder from her and then bent down to kiss her.

"You okay, baby?" Saint asked as he caressed her cheek.

"Yeah. I know it's bad, but it hits you differently when the evidence is in your face, right?"

We moved to the couch because guessing by the look on her face, we had another clue. I sat with her on my lap. Saint took a seat next to us, and Cal dragged the stool and sat in front of us.

"What are we looking at here, baby?" he asked as he caressed her thigh with his hands, making her squirm against my semi-hard cock. "We've seen these files before, but nothing made sense to us."

"You see that file that mentions the Strauss Foundation?" She pointed to the paper, and Cal nodded. He knew those papers better than any of us. He had spent countless hours staring at them, hoping to make a connection between the old man's murder and Erick's disappearance.

"Yeah, we looked into it," Cal said. "It's a private corporation. Nothing significant was found on it."

"That's the thing," she whispered. "When I first moved to America, my uncle had a visitor, and that person was referred to as Mr. Strauss."

"So you're saying that it's a person?" I asked.

"Well, that's what they referred to him by. That was the only time he came to the house, and my uncle wasn't happy about it. When he left, I asked if he was an associate from the school…"

Everly paused and took a deep breath.

"My uncle said that he ran a private organization that helped people in need match with a potential donor."

We were all silent for a fraction of a second. There it was; the missing piece that proved to us that they were in the flesh selling business.

"I mean, we guessed this, didn't we?" Saint added sadly.

"Yeah," Cal said.

"That's not all," Everly went on.

She took the page where we had all the codes. We weren't sure what they meant, it was just numbers and letters. "I think I know how to decode them."

Saint leaned over and rested his head on her tits. I glared at him because he caused her to squish me. "How were you able to figure that out so fast? Not that I don't think you're smart, but we never cracked it. Callum never cracked it."

No one could get mad at Saint, he wasn't malicious.

"Easy." Everly smiled at him and pinched his cheek.

"These are zip codes," she beamed.

And the three of us looked at her in awe.

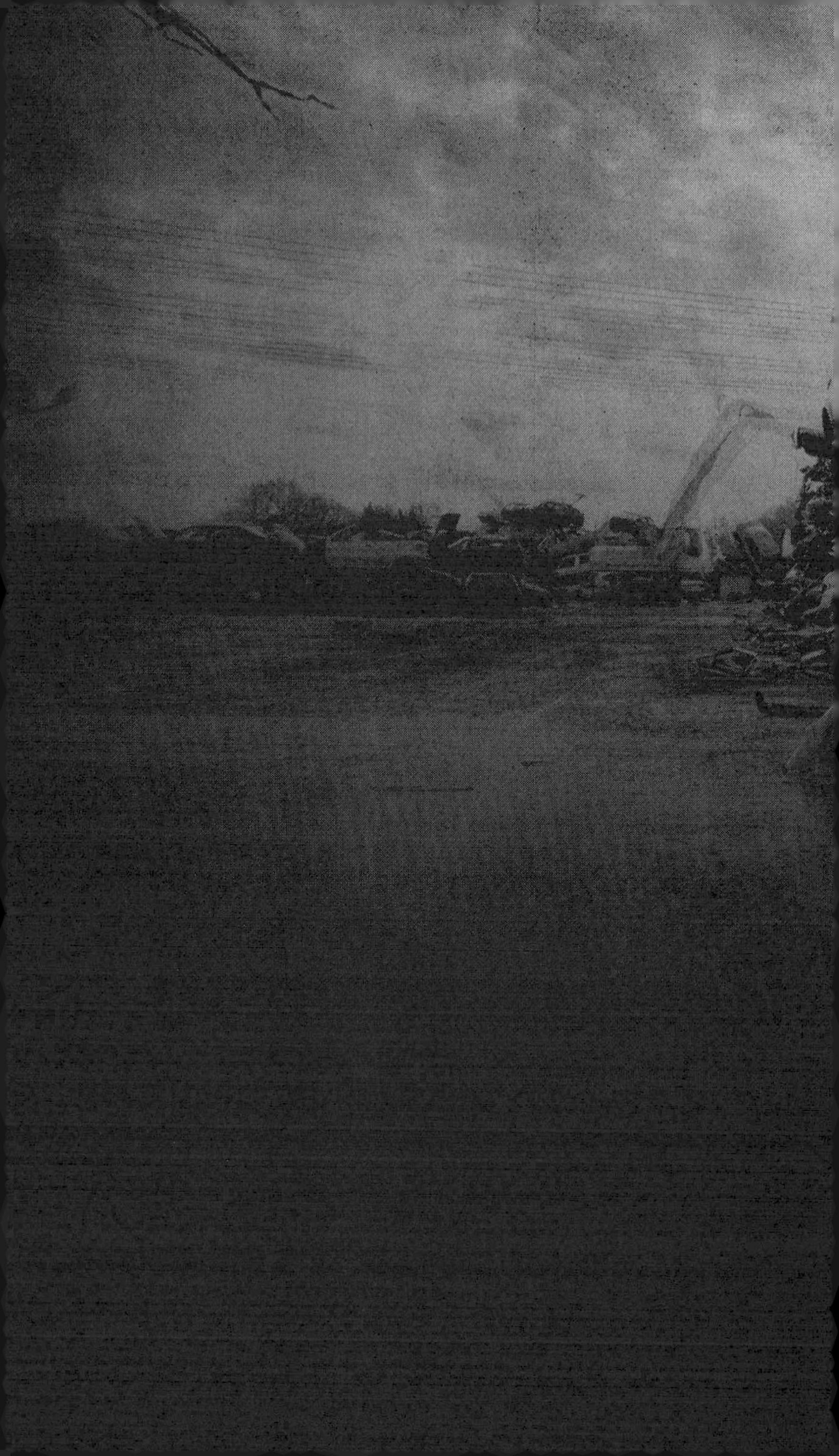

20

CALLUM

She'd done it. Our girl had cracked the code, in literally five seconds flat. The number of times I'd studied it, over and over again, and it hadn't made any sense. Everly never failed to amaze us, and now we had a real lead.

It appeared that our luck was changing. And that was even more apparent when my phone sounded with a text less than five minutes later.

I scanned quickly through the brief message. "We've got the information. The account numbers from the mayor's house—they've been traced."

"And?" Saint gestured impatiently with his hand when the silence had gone on for too long.

"And, it's too sensitive to send over the internet. There's too much risk of it being intercepted, I guess—it's not like we're hackers with knowledge of firewalls and whatever shit they use."

"So how do we get it?" Everly leaned forward, placing her hand over the top of the one I still had placed on her thigh. I turned my palm up, sliding my fingers between hers and giving her hand a reassuring squeeze, which made a small smile appear on her face.

"I need to meet a guy to get it. They've sent me a maps location." Hitting the link, I waited for the map to load, then zoomed out so I could see the area. "This is near Tiff's trailer park."

"You're not coming," Mateo said immediately, giving Saint a hard look. I was in complete agreement with him. We needed to keep Saint as far away from that bitch as possible.

"I'll go alone, and I need to leave now." Releasing Everly's hand, I climbed to my feet. "I'll be as quick as I can. You guys work on the zip codes. Now we know what they are, that should give us another lead."

Everly slid off Mateo's lap and came to stand in front of me. "I'm coming with you. I promise I'll stay safe—I'll wait inside the truck while you do what you need to. I just... I need to get out for a bit. Just drive, you know?"

I slowly nodded, because I did know. Glancing at Mateo and Saint over the top of Everly's head, I noted their resigned expressions. We all got it. And who were we to deny our girl the freedom she was craving? I calculated that the risk was minimal—our contact could be trusted, and on that open highway, we'd easily see if anyone was tailing us. Not that I expected anyone to be.

"Come on then. But you have to promise to stay in the truck."

Everly smiled, her expression lighter than I'd seen it in a while, and fuck, I wanted her to always look that way. "I promise. Let's go."

She stepped up to Mateo, then Saint, to say goodbye, which, to no one's surprise, ended up with Saint attempting to turn their goodbye hug into a groping session. I punched him lightly on the arm, tugging her away from him. "There'll be time for that later, but now, we need to get to work."

He shot me a grin, and I just shook my head at him, biting back my own smile.

"We'll be back as soon as we can," I told them. "Stay safe."

We'd only been driving for about ten minutes when I realized that there was a dark red sedan that seemed to be making all the same turns as I was. Keeping one eye on my rear-view mirror, I took the next left, which led to the local high school. The sedan followed, and when I turned left, then left again, ending up on the original street, it was still behind us.

"Fuck," I muttered. "Someone's following us. I'm gonna try and shake them, okay?"

Everly nodded, her mouth set in a flat line as I floored the accelerator, steering the truck toward a residential area. My phone beeped at me to tell me it was recalculating our route, but I didn't bother sparing it a glance—my priority right now was to shake this car.

Scanning the street we'd turned into, I made a decision. "If I can get a clear view of the plate, can you text it to the others?"

"Of course." Everly's fingers were poised over her phone screen before I'd even finished speaking. Lifting my foot from the gas pedal, I slowed the car right down, so the red sedan's front bumper almost kissed the back of my truck. I reeled off the number plate to Everly, then attempted to get a look at the driver. He had on dark glasses and a black hat, and I didn't recognize him. Probably one of the mayor's goons. When he saw me studying him, he pulled back, and the timing was perfect, because I floored my truck again, sending both Everly and myself jerking forward.

"Shit, sorry." I spun the wheel, sending the truck down one of the smaller side streets, counting the houses under my breath.

"It's okay." Everly's small hand landed on my leg, and she squeezed. It was the wrong time for my cock to wake up, given our current situation, but Everly seemed to have a direct line to it. "Anything I can help you with?" She trailed her fingers teasingly up my thigh, and when I groaned, frustrated that nothing could come of it, she laughed. "Maybe later. Just trying to take your mind off our stalker. Did we lose him?"

"Not yet, but we will. Hold on, it's gonna get bumpy." I trained my eyes on the mirror as I continued counting down the houses. When I got to the twenty-third house, I made a sudden right. The truck bumped up over a raised, gravelly area, and then we were heading down a small lane that I knew from experience was just about wide enough to accommodate us, although it was a close fit. The lane spat us out onto another residential street, and I took another left, counting the houses again until we got to another lane. When we were out the other side, I spun the wheel to the left, and kept driving, eventually reaching the outskirts of Blackstone, and then we were finally on the highway, heading for the meeting point.

Everly relaxed back against the seat when it was clear that we'd lost our pursuer. She lowered the window all the way down and turned the music up, and with her there next to me, tapping her fingers on the side of the car door in time with the music, I could almost kid myself that we were two normal people, young and carefree and reckless.

If only.

We passed the entrance to Saint's mom's trailer park, and then my phone announced that our destination was coming up on the right. There was a small truck stop up ahead, and I pulled into it, steering around the side of the building in an attempt to hide my truck from the road. When we came to a stop, I turned to Everly.

"I shouldn't be long. Stay here, out of sight. Any problems, call me straight away, okay?"

She nodded, then leaned forward, grabbing the back of my neck and pulling me to her. I went willingly, kissing her soft lips and threading my fingers through her hair.

"Stay safe," she murmured when I managed to tear myself away.

"I will."

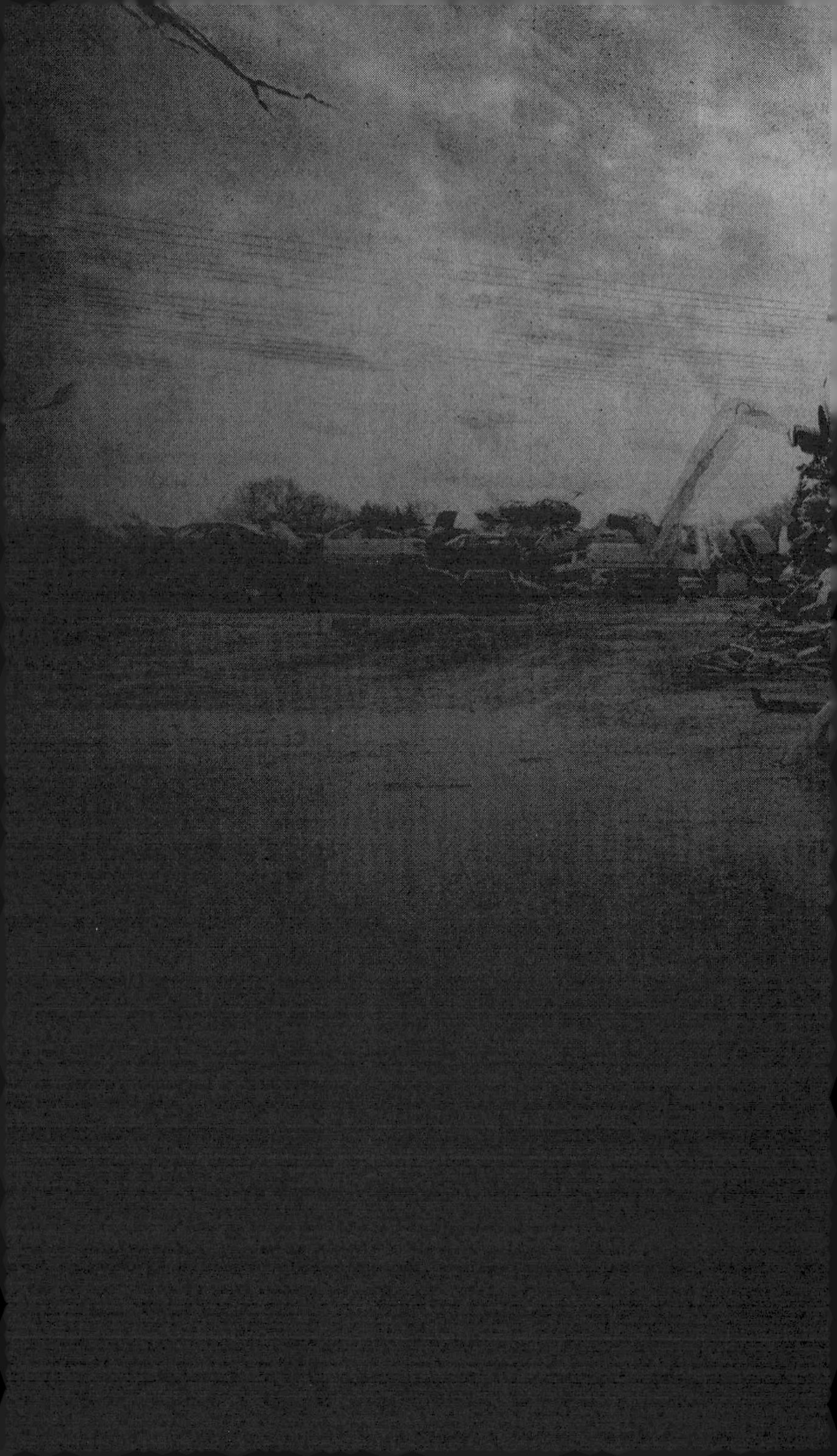

21

EVERLY

Leaning back against the headrest, I closed my eyes. I rubbed my thumb across my butterfly ring, taking comfort in the familiar feel, as my mind swirled with thoughts. What was my uncle's endgame with me? It was highly unlikely that he'd let me off that easily. I needed to think like him, to anticipate his moves, and try to stay ahead of him in this game of chess we were playing.

What did we know? I'd had a sick feeling in my stomach ever since the Strauss Foundation had been mentioned. Put it together with the fact that Erick had been missing body parts when he was found, and the moving lump I'd seen that night in the abandoned church, which now I was almost positive had been a person, and it painted a gruesome picture.

There was no doubt that our odds were long. These people had money and power, and I knew they'd do anything to protect their secret. The fact that I was a blood relative of my uncle, and therefore high profile, had probably been the thing that saved me. If I'd been anyone else... It didn't even bear thinking about.

And yet here we were, trying to take them down, to get justice for Erick and Dave. Were we crazy to try? Undoubtedly. But I knew that the four of us were committed to seeing this through, whatever it took.

Glancing at my phone, I realized that Callum had been gone for over twenty minutes. How long did it take to complete a handover of information? He'd told me to wait in the truck, and I'd planned to, but now I couldn't stop the worry from surging up within me. What if something had happened to him? I'd never forgive myself if there was something I could have done to prevent it.

My mind made up, I grabbed the keys from the ignition and exited the truck, locking the doors behind me. With my phone in one hand, and my keys in the other, I made my way around the side of the truck stop, ducking down when I reached the windows. Hopefully no one noticed me, because I knew I looked suspicious.

I reached the corner of the building and peered around it. There was a black car at one of the gas pumps, but other than that, there was no one around.

The sense of foreboding grew, and my heart was beating out of my chest. Where was Callum?

I risked a glance inside, and exhaled with relief. I could just about see Callum in the corner of the small diner that made up part of the truck stop building, with his hood up, shadowing his face. There was a guy sitting opposite him, also hooded, with a ball cap pulled down low on his head.

Shaking my head at my own paranoia, I turned to go back to the truck, but a flash of red caught my eye. Suddenly frozen in place, I watched in horror as a dark red sedan swung into the truck stop.

Fuck.

I ran. Straight for the truck. I had no idea how they'd

found us here—after we'd managed to lose them, and with the truck parked out of sight of the road—but they had. And Callum was inside. I had to lead them away from him. If he was caught with the sensitive information that he was being handed, we would be completely screwed.

Fumbling with the keys, I managed to get the truck open and climbed into the driver's seat. It took me a minute to adjust things so that my feet could reach the pedals, and I swore under my breath at the wasted time. Quickly adjusting the rear-view mirror, I jammed the key into the ignition and started up the engine.

The truck came to life with a roar, and I put it into reverse, driving it backward as fast as I dared, until it was out the front of the truck stop. The red sedan had been rolling slowly across the forecourt, but when I came into view, it came to a sudden stop.

That's it. Follow me. Don't look inside the diner. I carefully edged the truck toward the highway. It was scary, driving this huge beast of a machine after my low-slung, responsive Camaro, but I could handle it. I *had* to handle it. I had no choice.

Lucky for both me and my pursuer, the highway was quiet, and as I hit the gas, swinging into the road, the sedan followed me with ease.

The last thing I saw in my mirror before I left the truck stop behind was Callum bursting out of the diner's door, and I crossed my fingers that the driver of the sedan hadn't caught sight of him too.

Driving with one hand and keeping both eyes on the road, I hit the Call button on my phone, knowing that my last called number was likely to be one of the Boneyard Kings.

"Everly." Mateo's smooth voice came through the speaker. "Already—"

"There's someone chasing me and Callum's stuck at the truck stop and I can't drive this truck and I'm really scared." I was almost hyperventilating, and only the knowledge that if I didn't keep control of this truck, I was likely to seriously injure myself or even get myself killed, stopped me from tipping over the edge.

"Hey. Slow down. What's happening?"

My voice shaking, I repeated what I'd just said, adding that the car had trailed us through Blackstone, but Callum had been able to shake it.

"Shit. Someone must've put a tracker on the truck. Those fuckers!" I heard Saint shout, followed by the sound of something heavy smashing against the wall.

"We're coming. We're taking the Camaro." Mateo's voice stayed low and soothing. "You can do this, baby."

"I d-don't know what to do."

The noise of my Camaro's engine starting up filtered through the speaker as Mateo replied. "Keep driving for now. Which direction are you headed?"

"Away from Blackstone."

"Okay. There's an exit about two miles past the truck stop. Take it, then go over the top, and get back on the highway. Head for Tiff's place. Can you do that for me?"

"Y-yes."

"We'll meet you there. I'll give Cal a call and update him. He's better off staying where he is for now, so don't try to stop to get him or anything, okay? Just go straight to Tiff's."

"Okay."

"Want me to stay on the phone?"

I shook my head, then remembered he couldn't see me. "No. It's okay. I need all my concentration to do this."

"You can do it. We have faith in you, baby."

As soon as the call ended, I gripped the wheel with both hands, breathing hard. The sedan hadn't caught up to me yet, but it was only a matter of time.

I had to make it to Tiff's place before that happened.

The exit sign loomed up ahead, and I crossed my fingers, said a silent prayer, and left the highway.

22

MATEO

The fear in Everly's voice had goosebumps rising on my arms as soon as I answered her call. I didn't hesitate to put the phone on speaker. Saint reached for the keys to the Camaro, and we ran to it as I tried to be as calm as I could for Everly.

She was all alone, and right now there was nothing Callum could do. Even though we would have much rather blown our cover and protected her, she took that choice away, and as much as we beat ourselves up over that shit, there was no denying that it felt nice. To have someone want to risk their life for you was beautiful.

"We get one step forward and those fuckers sprint to the front," Saint hissed as he looked out the window.

I was driving as fast as I could to not draw attention to us, and I knew we both wished I could go faster. It was the only reason he wasn't making a comment on it.

"You know, I was always grateful Tiff didn't live closer or else she would be making home visits for cash," Saint said. "But now it seems like she's a whole town away."

Desperation did that to you. It replayed the worst

moments of your lives, and instead of minutes, it lasted hours.

"Just stay calm," I said as I gripped the steering wheel. "Our girl is smart."

He tipped his head just a fraction.

"Funny," he snorted humorlessly. "You didn't want me to go near Tiff, and yet here we all are."

Somehow that bitch had all the luck. We knew Tiff only ever rung Saint up for cash. So we also knew money was going to be tight for him, with him paying both his frat dues and his share of the new camera equipment.

We didn't mind giving him the money, we just hated that it went to Tiffany.

"It's okay," I said. "Just drop off the money and leave."

Because he had such a kind heart, not giving her anything fucked with his mind.

As soon as we got on the deserted road that led to the trailer, I gassed it. We came to a stop in front of Tiff's trailer, but there was no sign of our girl yet.

I left the car in park and got out.

"Switch with me, and as soon as she comes take her home," I let him know.

It didn't take long before I heard the engine of our truck. Then I saw Everly, and fuck she looked terrified, but I knew she could do it.

She parked the car, forgetting to turn off the engine, and ran out. She threw herself in my arms. I soothed her the best I could. Time was not on our side right now.

"You did great, baby," I whispered as I kissed the top of her head. "Go with Saint."

She tipped her head, and I could see unshed tears. Probably the crash of the adrenaline kicking in.

I grabbed the back of her head and pulled her in for a

kiss. My mouth crashed against hers. Her hands came to my chest and fisted the material of my shirt.

"Everything is going to be okay," I murmured against her lips.

"Where are you going?"

"To get Cal," I told her.

She stood straighter, her eyes hardening.

"Shouldn't we all go together?"

I heard the door opening, and I knew Saint was coming to get her since time wasn't on our side.

"If we do, what you just did would have been for nothing."

She bit her lip, hating my answer but knowing it had to be done. She pulled away from me and went with Saint while I ran to the truck. Without looking at them, because I knew she was safe in Saint's arms, I turned the truck around and left, calling Callum as I did so.

"Is she with you?" Cal asked in a frantic voice.

If any of us would have been in his position, we would have been desperate too. To know the best option was to sit still fucking killed.

"She's freaked out but okay," I told him. "I left her with Saint. I switched the cars. I'll come get you."

"They fucking tracked us," he hissed.

"I bet anything it was after the pig fucking stopped us."

"Yeah, they don't like it that we're around her, and that's going to make them reckless."

"I know," I admitted.

"Be careful," Cal warned before hanging up.

There was no sign of the car just yet. If they were smart, they were going to regroup somewhere else. Or maybe see what we would do.

We couldn't get confident because if I knew anything,

that was what they wanted.

I was barely coming to a stop when Callum was already running toward me.

"Did they follow you?" he asked.

"Not that I noticed," I told him.

"We need to get rid of this shit fast, and more than that, we need to send them a fucking message. You don't touch our girl and get away with it."

I gripped the steering wheel tighter. Now that they were both safe, the fear had faded, and all that remained was anger.

"What if we use Lorenzo?"

Callum grinned. "I was thinking the same thing."

We kept our eyes on the road, but there was no sign of the sedan. While I drove, Cal updated Everly and Saint on our plan.

The info he had received was going to have to wait just a little longer while we took care of business. We had waited almost a decade; we could wait a couple of hours.

We made it to the place where the fights were held. It was early, so no one was around, but anyone tracking us and looking at the location was bound to know just who this place belonged to.

Callum and I got to work right away, him on the hood as I got on the ground.

"Anything?" he asked.

"No." I replied.

When we were sure nothing was there, we got to work on the interior, then the cabin.

"What the fuck is going on?" I said, annoyed.

Callum was thinking as he looked at our truck. We looked at each other, and then it dawned on us.

"Motherfucker," Cal spat.

23

SAINT

Caring about people meant that you allowed room for fear. I thought that was why a lot of people were scared to love. They didn't want that crippling feeling that came with caring for others.

That was how I felt when I thought of Everly and my brothers. I had a deep-rooted fear of losing them. But now, standing in front of that old trailer, I couldn't say the same shit for Tiff.

With her, it was the opposite. I dreaded the moment she called. To hear her voice on the other end of the line. I knew, deep down, it had always killed me that to her I wasn't a son. I was just a money cow.

Everly and I were inside the Camaro as Mateo went to pick up Callum. Now that the fucking goons had stopped taking us by surprise, I doubted they would try anything. Going to Lorenzo's grounds to get rid of the bug was a power play. Let them make their own assumptions.

If they feared our connection with Everly, adding Lorenzo to the mix was bound to make them shit their pants.

"How are you feeling?" I asked Everly, my hand going to her thigh and massaging it.

"Better now." She smiled weakly at me. "It was fucking scary."

I pulled her into my lap.

"You did great, baby," I whispered against her cheek. "We're still mad that you put yourself at risk—"

She cut me off with a glare.

"What was I supposed to do, lead them to Cal? How can I sit back and do nothing when you guys would do anything for me?"

She had a point, but the thought of her getting hurt would send us into a tailspin.

"Shouldn't we get going?" she said after a little bit, but her eyes wandered to the side.

We were in front of Tiff's trailer, after all.

"Do you need me to come with you?" she asked.

I looked at her. And then I looked at the trailer and shook my head. I liked that she offered, but this was something I needed to do on my own.

"No, baby. This is something I must do on my own. I hate that you've seen that place. Just lock the doors and wait for me here, okay?"

She looked like she wanted to argue with me, but ultimately sat up and went to the passenger side. I missed her heat and comfort instantly.

I opened the car door and started to walk up the dirt path to what had been my sometimes childhood home. I didn't bother knocking and opened the dingy door. The place smelled like smoke and piss.

"Hello?" I called out.

There was no answer. And that dreadful feeling that was always there when I came to visit returned.

"You don't want the money?" I yelled.

Nothing.

My shoulders dropped and I sighed. I went in search of Tiff in her trashy bedroom, hoping like hell she had no company.

The door was one smack away from breaking. There she laid in the middle of her once white bed, sleeping.

Not bothering to wake her, I threw the bills on the bed. It wasn't like she wouldn't know where they came from. I was the only person giving her fucking money.

Sure, once upon a time she had been beautiful, but she was too coked out now that it had all faded.

Maybe rushing out had been a pussy move, but I just knew I would feel better away from this place, and my conscience would be clear.

Everly unlocked the car as soon as she saw me. Without words, she rested her head on my shoulder as I drove the hell away from that place.

"You want to talk about it?" she asked once we had put some distance between the trailers and us.

"Not really," I said.

She leaned up and kissed my cheek. "She's your mum, so we all understand."

I gripped the steering wheel. Life was bullshit. Here was Tiff, a bitch of a mother, and good people like Everly's mom died. It was unfair.

When we got to the house, it wasn't surprising that Cal and Mateo weren't there yet. Last update we had was that they were heading for the fighting grounds to get rid of the tracker.

"Come on, my little drag racer, let's get you inside," I teased her.

She glared at me but then smiled, relieved.

"You think they'll take long?" she asked.

"Hopefully not," I told her. "You hungry? I'm starving."

She lifted a quizzical brow.

"You can cook?"

I brought my hand up to my chest.

"I have many talents, my dear Everrrly. My dick and tongue game are just two of them."

She punched my arm and laughed, and the tension was leaving both of us.

We were in the kitchen, attempting to make some food, because now that Everly was safe and Tiff was dealt with, my dick was like, *it's my turn to have some fun*.

Everly was in front of me as I guided her on how to make my chili. Today called for a comfort meal. After the way our hearts were racing earlier, we needed to take it slow.

My hands were on her hips while I whispered in her ear to get the ingredients we needed. "These are the things we need to dice, and this is the stuff that will be minced."

She turned to look back at me with a surprised face. "Who are you?" she teased.

I picked her up and put her on the counter. "I know, it's hard to believe someone as perfect as me exists. Big dick, handsome, and can cook—that sounds like a wi—"

"A bunch of red flags, if you ask me."

We both turned around to look at the two people who had come in. Mateo and Callum stood on the other side where the hallway met the kitchen.

"I'm walking green flags," I spat at Mateo.

This time, it was Callum who answered, "Anyone who says they're a green flag is automatically a red flag."

I leaned in to give Everly a kiss, and then turned around

and flipped them both off. Everly jumped off the counter and ran to Callum's open arms.

He hugged her tight.

My chest felt warm and even though a lot of shit had gone down lately, I couldn't remember the last time this place felt like a real home.

"Because you're assholes, I'm not feeding you," I stated as I got back to dicing. I heard laughter and then the scraping of the chairs moving so we could have a family meal.

24

EVERLY

Everyone was acting normally, but I knew there was something wrong. Something Callum and Mateo weren't telling us.

Placing down the knife I'd been using to cut up the ingredients for the chili, I straightened up. Callum had his back to me, setting out cutlery on the table, but Mateo was facing me, and I met his gaze. "What's happened? Tell us."

Mateo shook his head. "Not now. Let's have a family dinner, then talk about it after."

The smile dropped from Saint's face, and he looked at Mateo, his brows pulling together. "Tell us now."

Callum turned around, and exchanged glances with Mateo, then he said simply, "The truck didn't have a tracker on it."

"It was a clean swoop," Mateo added. "Nothing out of the ordinary."

"So how did they find us? Was it just a coincidence?" I stared at them, hoping against hope that it *was* a coincidence, although deep down, I knew it wasn't.

"We don't know for sure," Callum rubbed his hand

across his face. "But we don't think it was a coincidence. The chances of the car that had been tailing us following us all the way to that exact same truck stop... it had to be purposeful. We thought that maybe they'd managed to plant a tracker on one of us."

Saint gasped out loud and rushed over to me, grabbing my hand. Before I even had a chance to react, he was tugging my butterfly ring from my finger.

"This!" He held the ring up, and it only took a few seconds for comprehension to dawn on all our faces.

Of course. Why hadn't I thought of it before? I knew there was no way my uncle was going to let this go quietly. Which meant he'd known every single move I'd made since he gave me the ring back. He knew where I'd been, and by extension, he would've known who I'd been with—because why would I be spending so much time at the junkyard, if not to spend time with the Boneyard Kings? As far as he was aware, my Camaro had been scrapped, so I didn't even have that as an excuse. Not to mention, I'd obviously spent my nights here, and that was something that couldn't be explained away.

My eyes filled with tears, and I leaned against the counter, placing my head in my hands. "I'm so sorry, guys. I put us all in danger."

I heard the three of them murmuring quietly to each other, and then arms came around my body.

"Hey. It's not your fault." Saint kissed the top of my head. "How would you have known? None of us even thought about it."

I hugged him back tightly, letting his words soothe me. He stroked up and down my back until I was calmer, then when I drew back to look up at him, he gave me a soft smile.

"It's all gonna be okay. Cal and Matty have gone to the

workshop—there's some tools in there they can use to, uh, take apart the ring to check for a tracker. They'll be careful with it, though. I promise. We know how important it is to you."

"Thanks," I sniffed. "I just wish I'd realized sooner."

"We'll sort it out." Releasing me, he picked up my knife. "Let's finish making this chili, okay?"

"Okay."

By the time the chili was almost finished simmering in the pot, the spices permeating the air and making my stomach rumble, Callum and Mateo had returned.

"We found the tracker," Mateo announced, walking over to me and handing me my ring. "That fucker had hidden it under the black stone."

"I can't believe he did that." Holding up the ring, I examined it. They'd clearly taken care with it, because it looked just the same as normal—if anything, it was shinier than usual. "Thank you for putting it back together for me."

He took the ring back from me and slid it onto my finger. "Anything for you, mamas. Cal and I spoke, and we think you should keep the tracker in your purse. Your uncle knows you're here with us—that much will have become clear in the time he's been tracking you. If you have it in your purse, going to and from classes, but leave your purse in the house the rest of the time, he won't know where else you're going. Any other times we need to meet up with Lorenzo here, or anyone else who's working with us, we can work something out so it'll look like you're somewhere else when that happens."

"Okay. I guess that makes sense. For now."

"For now," he agreed. "Just until we know more. We'll keep you safe, Everly. You can count on us."

Then he lowered his head to mine and kissed me. I

wound my arms around his neck, kissing him back, opening my mouth to him and feeling his tongue stroke against mine. When the kiss ended, we were both breathing hard, and I could feel the hard outline of his cock pressing into me.

"Mmm. You taste so good." His gorgeous brown eyes were wide and dark, and he licked his lips as he stared down at me.

"So do you." I wanted nothing more than for the four of us to go to bed and forget everything else, but I knew everyone was hungry and crashing after the adrenaline from earlier, so it would have to wait.

For now.

"What about the information you got from the guy at the truck stop, Cal?" Turning in Mateo's arms, I leaned back against him, facing the others.

At last, a smile appeared on Callum's face. "We've got a whole list of names and locations. I bet anything that if we cross-reference them with those zip codes from the folder, we'll find matches." He looked pointedly at where Mateo's arms were wrapped around me. "I know what you're thinking, and we all want it too. But first, we eat. Then we cross-reference this information. We need to get answers, and fast. We're running out of time."

Stepping over to me, he grinned at Mateo, and then lowered his head to my ear. His voice came out as a low, sexy rasp that sent a delicious shiver through me. "After that, baby, we fuck."

25

MATEO

As soon as we finished eating, the dreadful feeling we had been pushing away since we got back reappeared.

You couldn't avoid bad news, just prolong it.

The feeling was there, but not as intense as before. What we did today was nice—no, it felt right. It was that same warm feeling we used to get when the old man was here. There was a sense of belonging that had been missing from our lives.

Finding Everly's ring tracker pissed us off like no other, but if her uncle wanted to play games, we would use it against him.

Now the four of us were laying on the floor in the old man's room. It was weird to continue to call it that. He wasn't even here and hadn't been for a long time. He didn't ask us to keep his room as some sort of shrine.

"You need to stop moping," the old man said as he came into Saint's room.

It was the first year following Erick's death and although we were grateful to be out of the system, we still carried the guilt that we got out and he didn't.

We all had our own rooms, but today we just hung out in Saint's. There was an unexplainable need to be near one another. None of us voiced it, but we felt it. Death was funny that way. Although it took from you, it made the ones left behind want to hold on tighter.

We all looked at the old man, not knowing what to say to him.

"Best way you can honor a dead person is to keep a hold of the things they loved most. Mourn them, follow their legacy, but let them go."

Maybe neither Erick nor the old man would want us to go down this path because this wasn't their legacy and they wanted us out of harm's way, but I thought deep down they would understand, especially if we helped others.

"We should clear out his room," I said out loud, and three sets of confused eyes looked at me, since we were all ready to see the papers.

"Throw everything out?" Saint questioned.

"It's long overdue," Cal agreed.

"I'm not saying throw everything, but we can't keep this as a shrine. He wouldn't have wanted that."

Everly reached out and touched Saint's hand. She was sitting between Cal and I and across from him.

Saint sighed. "It'll take me a minute to be able to have sex in here without feeling like the old man is watching me."

Both Cal and I gave him questioning looks.

"We can set up that California king we ordered here. It's the biggest room. Has a decent closet."

That wasn't a bad idea.

"And you all get to have your own rooms if you piss me off." Everly grinned.

I didn't think she realized what she said or what it meant to us, but the fact that she could see herself in our home—that meant the world.

Based on the looks on my brothers' faces, we were all in the same boat. We were in love with her.

"Let's get this over with," Cal managed to say.

"Yes, and then we can fuck."

We all laughed while Saint threw one hand in the air, the other one behind his back for balance, and began to hump the air.

"Okay, let's get this over with," I said as I reached for the papers. Whatever was on these was going to be fucked up.

Everly used our computer while we cross-examined the papers.

"These addresses are all over the state, but some of them are in neighboring ones too," Everly whispered, and the lump in my throat got bigger.

I looked at the papers we got from the guy, a descriptive transcript with no names but characteristics, and then I looked at a file we had printed on information from the disappearance page. Basic information on those who were never found. Sure enough, it matched.

This was the perfect setup. People who had no one to claim them, who were healthy, and were considered a waste of space by some. Then you had the rich with deep pockets, willing to pay anything for a chance to live, not caring how that chance came to be.

"Fuck," Saint hissed, almost in pain. "It's here."

Cal reached for the paper. He read it to himself and then looked at us with a somber expression.

"Boy. Caucasian. 11 years old. Blood type O-. Healthy kidneys, liver, and lungs."

We all felt like we were going to fucking throw up.

I reached and took the paper from Cal, because that could be anyone, but then it had a zip code and a number. The air left my lungs. Props to the fucking dean for being so fucking organized. It was the location of the foster house.

"We are bringing him down, no matter what," I spat, throwing the papers in the center.

The mood was somber mixed with anger. All I could think of was how much Erick must have suffered before he passed away. He didn't deserve that shit. Not one person on that list did.

The world was a cruel place.

26

CALLUM

It was the proof we'd been looking for, and it made me fucking sick. We were dealing with people with no moral code. People who had no problem with murder, just so that they could live. They had the blood of innocents on their hands, and everyone involved needed to be brought down.

The dean, the mayor, and the police chief would pay.

"They know that we're onto them. Even if they're unsure of exactly how much we know, they're suspicious enough to be tracking Everly's movements. We got her out of the church, so they know we're aware of that location, which I think we can all agree was where they kept their victims before transporting them..." I trailed off, unwilling to voice aloud what we all knew happened once these innocent people were taken away.

"These people are monsters." Everly's eyes filled with tears, but she straightened up, a determined look on her face. "We *will* stop them."

"We will." I began stacking the papers. "We need to

come up with a plan, and we're gonna need Lorenzo on board."

"Are we done for the day?" Saint handed me the papers closest to him. "'Cause I have a bottle of Jack with our names on it, and I was promised sex."

His words came across as flippant, but I knew that it was just his way of lightening the atmosphere. He cared just as deeply as the rest of us did. He was right, anyway. Things were so fucking dark and depressing, we needed a break from it, to remind ourselves of the good.

And there was no fucking way that I'd turn down sex with our girl.

"Yeah. I'll clear this up, you get the Jack, and we'll meet in my bedroom."

"Why does it have to be your bedroom?" Saint pouted, and I rolled my eyes.

"Because you haven't changed your sheets, and I don't know what I might catch."

"Hey, I got tested weeks ago! We all did! I've got a clean bill of health." He tried to shove his phone in my face, probably to show me his test results, but I knocked his arm away.

"Even so. My bedroom."

When I made it to my room, I stopped in the doorway, taking in the scene in front of me.

Everly was standing next to the bed, facing the full-length mirror that was on the wall. From behind her, a shirtless Mateo was sliding his arms around her waist and lifting her shirt. He slowly exposed her beautiful body, murmuring to her in Spanish that I knew she didn't understand, but fucking turned her on, if the way she was moaning against him was anything to go by. When her shirt was off, he smoothed down her hair and started kissing her neck, and she arched her body back against him, rolling her ass against his dick. He groaned, undoing her bra with one hand before sliding it off, then gripped her lightly around the throat.

In the mirror, I had a perfect view of her gorgeous tits, topped by her pink, pebbled nipples.

So fucking hot.

I palmed my rapidly hardening cock, watching them both, feeling the anticipation building in the air. As Mateo's hands slid onto Everly's tits, I heard him murmur, "Watch yourself." She stared into the mirror, her cheeks flushed and her mouth open in an O. Her pupils were wide, and she looked so fucking turned on that I had to grip onto the door-frame to stop myself from going over there.

"Fuck, that's hot. Why aren't you joining? You could take someone's eye out with your dick." Saint's voice sounded close to my ear.

"Yeah, speak for yourself." I pointedly looked down where he was sporting a boner you could see from space. And he was naked already. "I'm not joining yet. I want to watch."

He stared at me, and then back at them. "I see the appeal. Any objections if I join them?"

"Go for it."

"Don't mind if I do. You might wanna take care of your dick situation. I think you're strangling it."

"Fuck off. Go and join them." Now that he mentioned it, the way my dick was straining against my sweats was a little uncomfortable. And when Everly's gaze met mine in the mirror, full of heat, I knew what to do.

As Saint crossed the room and dropped to his knees in

front of her, I lifted my shirt over my head, slowly, like I was doing a fucking striptease or something. Flexing my muscles as I raised it higher, I watched Everly lick her lips, her gaze fixated on me.

Saint unbuttoned her jeans and slid them down her legs, and Mateo's hands began to caress her tits. Her eyes fluttered closed for a second, and when they opened again, her gaze raked over the three of us, and she moaned.

Fuuuck. I threw my shirt to the floor, watching the three of them. Mateo was grinding himself against Everly's ass as he got his hands all over her tits, and Saint was kissing up her legs. Everly had one hand in Saint's hair, and the other was thrown back, holding Mateo's head against her throat as he sucked a hickey into her creamy skin.

I lowered my hands to the waistband of my sweats. Everly gasped as Saint's mouth reached her pussy, kissing her over the damp fabric of her underwear. Almost as if we'd planned it, as I began to lower my sweats, Saint got his hands on Everly's underwear. Her gaze flitted between what Saint was doing and what I was doing, and when both of us were fully naked, moans echoed around the room.

My cock was fucking throbbing, and my balls were heavy and just about ready to explode, but I didn't touch them yet. I waited, watching Saint hook one of Everly's legs over his shoulder, and then put his mouth on her soaked pussy. Fuck, she was so wet for us, I could see it from here.

Mateo seemed to have had enough of being the only one who wasn't fully naked, and he stopped playing with Everly's tits long enough to shove down his sweats. When his cock was free, he angled himself so he could slide it between her legs, thrusting like he was already fucking her.

I couldn't take it any longer. I stalked over to my nightstand where I kept lube, pumped some out, then wrapped my hand around my cock.

I groaned low in my throat. After all that buildup, even just having my hand on myself was so fucking pleasurable. I knew there was no way I was going to last. Saint was already jerking himself as he ate Everly out, and Mateo's thrusts were getting harder.

Stepping up to them, I met Everly's eyes in the mirror.

"Cal," she moaned. "Come for me."

"Fuck, Everly. *Fuck*." My cock throbbed in my grip as I came, hot ropes of cum covering my hand and jetting onto Everly's naked body.

"You want a cock inside you, mamas?" Mateo's eyes were almost black, he was so aroused. She nodded, and I stepped right up to her.

"Use my cum as lube."

Mateo pulled back a little, and I slid my hand down to her ass, spreading my cum around her hole, then pushing one cum-covered finger inside her. Adding another finger, I opened her up, scissoring my fingers inside her, until she was tapping on my arm.

"Enough. Need. Mateo."

It said a lot about the closeness of our relationship that he slid his hand over mine, smearing the remainder of my release onto his own hand, then began working his hand over his cock. Then he bent her over, getting her to place her hands on the wall on either side of the mirror, and pushed inside her. Saint angled his body down so he could continue to taste her as his hand worked his cock faster, and as Mateo slid all the way inside, he came, painting my bedroom floor with his cum.

27

EVERLY

Saint's mouth working over my pussy, now joined by his fingers, and Mateo's cock buried inside my ass, were sending me spiraling toward the edge. Watching Callum watch us had been one of the hottest moments of my life, and when he'd come just from watching us? I'd almost orgasmed right then.

I knew it wouldn't be long until I did. How did I get so lucky, to have three hot guys who knew exactly how to pleasure me, to keep me so satisfied that I knew I'd never want anyone else?

Saint twisted his fingers at the same time as Mateo gave a hard thrust, and I shattered with a cry, falling over the edge. As I shuddered against Mateo's body, Saint's tongue never letting up, drawing out my orgasm, I felt Mateo coming inside me, his hot breaths panted against my neck as he filled me up.

"Wow."

That was the only word I could manage when I eventually came down from my high. Mateo slowly withdrew from me, and then Saint climbed to his feet, lifting me up and carrying me to the bed.

Letting my eyes fall closed, I relaxed back against the pillows. A soft, wet cloth was gently dragged across my overheated skin, and I smiled, letting my guys take care of me. I heard Callum tell Saint that he had to clean up his cum from the carpet, otherwise there'd be consequences, and it made my smile widen.

The bed dipped next to me, and Callum's voice sounded in my ear. "You want to sleep now, baby? You can sleep here."

I nodded slowly. "Sleep sounds good."

That was the last thing I remembered. When I woke, the moon was shining brightly through the window. No one had remembered to close the blinds, and the room was illuminated by moonlight. The window was open a crack, letting in the night breeze, making the room the perfect temperature. Callum was fast asleep next to me on his stomach, looking softer and younger in his sleep than he normally did, with all his stresses melted away. Mateo and Saint had disappeared, I guessed to their own bedrooms. I knew that all of us were looking forward to the day we had a bed big enough for us all to sleep in comfortably.

Glancing at Callum's nightstand, I saw that it was just after two a.m. What had woken me? I never normally woke in the middle of the night unless I'd had a nightmare about my parents dying, but tonight I'd been sleeping peacefully.

Clink.

I might've missed the sound if the window had been closed, but as it was, the faint noise carried over the night breeze.

Carefully climbing out of the bed so I didn't disturb Callum, I made my way over to the window, scanning the outside area. I couldn't see anything, but then, it was dark outside.

It could've been nothing important—an animal, probably—but something was telling me to check. Glancing back at Callum, I debated waking him up, but eventually I decided that it was better to. Even if it ended up being nothing, none of the Boneyard Kings would be happy with me going off on my own, now we were sure that the people we wanted to bring down knew I was here.

"Cal." Shaking his shoulder gently, I leaned down to whisper in his ear. I couldn't help pressing a soft kiss to his cheek, before saying his name again a little louder.

He groaned into the pillow, but then suddenly, he was wide awake, rolling his body to face me, his eyes alert and watchful. "What is it?"

"I heard a noise outside. It might be nothing, but I thought we should check."

He nodded, all business. "Okay. I'm going to check it out. Wait here. We'll wake the others if we need to."

"I'm coming with you," I said immediately.

"No, baby. Stay here. Or go wake up Mateo and Saint—if we're awake, then they can be awake too."

"Okay."

He gave me a quick kiss, then swung himself out of the bed, pulling on a pair of sweatpants, and then disappeared out of the door. I made my way to the hallway that led to Saint and Mateo's rooms, but my attention was caught by a soft curse coming from farther down the hallway

"Callum?" I whisper-shouted into the darkness.

"I'm okay." His voice came from a distance, but I heard it clearly, and I breathed a sigh of relief. My heart was still beating out of my chest, but at least I knew he was safe.

I wasted no time in waking up Mateo and Saint, and as I

explained the situation to them, a noise sounded clearly from outside, a thunk of something solid against metal. Mateo and Saint exchanged glances, and then ran for the front door, where Callum had already disappeared.

"Stay inside, and keep the door locked," Saint instructed me, closing the door behind him. I did as he said, flipping the lock, then making my way to the window to see if I could see anything. One of the guys had turned on the floodlights, which made some areas bright, but cast others into deep, dark shadows.

I caught a movement out of the corner of my eye, and I leaned closer to the window to get a better look.

Nothing was there.

There was another movement.

My heart pounded, and my breath caught in my throat.

The movement hadn't come from outside. It was a reflection in the window.

Slowly, I turned around. My mouth was dry, and I couldn't breathe.

I was trapped here in the house.

Raising my head, I faced the man. He looked so different to when I'd seen him last. His eyes were wild, his clothes were unkempt, and his hair was sticking out in different directions. But all of those things paled in comparison to the huge grin he had on his face. A grin that spoke of madness, of evil, of retribution.

"I couldn't have planned it any better. Little Everly Walker, all alone, with her three protectors on the other side of a locked door." His smile widened, and his eyes glittered feverishly. "Let the games begin."

28

SAINT

"I'm so tired," I whined.

Today had been one of the most draining days of my life. All I wanted was a good night's sleep to forget about everything those stupid papers talked about.

Now that I was awake, not even Everly's sweet taste could make it go away.

"It's probably nothing, but we should check it out," Callum said.

"You should have checked it out with Matty. Some of us need our beauty sleep."

Mateo used that moment to punch my arm —fucker.

I rubbed my arm. "It's not like I was lying," I mumbled.

"Can you two stop fucking around?" Callum bit out.

Someone was cranky without sleep.

"The faster we get this done, the sooner we can go back to bed."

He had a point. Hell, maybe by that time, we could go for round two. Suddenly I perked up.

"I'll check over there," Mateo said, already heading to the west side of the compound.

Callum went straight ahead. If anyone was where Everly thought she had heard activity, they would get lost in the maze. Leaving them to it, I went to the east side to check it out. With my phone in hand, I flashed the light around. Now that we were out here, I was thinking that it was probably stupid on our parts to come out unarmed. At the same time, we didn't think anyone would be stupid enough to come for us here.

The farther I walked away from the house, the worse I started to feel. It was an eerie feeling that was taking root.

The wind started to howl louder.

I moved closer until I was at the edge of the yard, but I couldn't see anything.

I jumped up when my phone rang. Looking at the caller ID, I sighed in relief.

"Anything?" Cal asked.

"Nope," I told him, taking one last look before deciding to go back.

"The maze looks clean. Call Mateo while I run through it."

He hung up, and I called Mateo as I walked back to the house.

"Nothing, you?" he greeted.

That feeling that was there got stronger.

"No, let's finish and head up."

I did one last sweep with the light, and not even a fucking rodent could be seen. When that was done, I started to run back to the house. When I got back to where we started, I went up to Cal's room from the outside. I flashed my light on the floor, trying to see if there were any prints, but there was nothing. I followed the path upward, and my heart fucking stopped when I came across a pair of legs. I brought my arm out, ready to swing.

"What the fuck are you doing?"

Fuck.

It was Mateo.

"Shit, nothing," I told him. "There's no evidence of any sort of breaking in on my end," I told him.

Just then, Callum could be seen through the shadows, running toward us.

"Nothing," he said, out of breath.

"Negative," Mateo told him, and I shook my head.

"Let's go in because Saint is scared," Mateo joked.

"Oh, fuck you, Matty. I was being Carmen fucking Sandiego trying to find clues. I even went to the window. You just caught me by surprise."

"What did Everly say?" Callum asked.

"What do you mean?" I asked, a little confused.

"She's in my room; she was probably peeking through the window," he said it like it was obvious.

The panicked look on my face must have made them uneasy.

I took off running, and I heard them come up behind me. Fuck, Cal was right, Everly would have been there trying to look at the backyard.

We made it back to Cal's room.

I felt like an idiot for not doing this before. I got there first. I peeked in through the window but saw no sign of Everly. She was probably in the living room.

"The front," Mateo said as Cal was already heading that way. I ran behind them. The front gate was closed, but that was not what my brothers were looking at.

We could barely make out a car that was parked between the grass and the road, all the way across from us.

We were all alone out here. No car should have been there. Whoever had parked there knew that we had cameras around, but they wanted to be close enough to come to us.

"Why didn't we fucking check the cameras?" I hissed the question that Cal and Mateo were probably already beating themselves over with.

"Let's just go inside," Cal told us.

Mateo pulled out his phone, probably checking the cameras as we spoke.

"Come on, go in." I gave Cal a gentle push.

"Anyone brought their key?" he asked us.

"Everly, baby, open the door!" I yelled as Cal knocked.

Mateo kept switching his focus between us and the phone. That anxious feeling was now dread. I hated how familiar it was starting to become. Once this all ended, this feeling better not fucking graze our lives again.

"Everly!" Callum yelled, this time sounding a little desperate.

There was no way she wasn't hearing us.

I pulled out my phone and called her.

"No answer."

Since I was the fastest, I ran back around the house, calling her phone, and once I got close to Callum's room, I could hear the sound of it ringing. Once I peeked in the window, I could see it flashing on the bed.

Fuck. I walked around the house, passing the windows of all our rooms to see if I could peek inside.

Sometimes, we didn't do good things, but that didn't mean we were shit people.

When I pulled back around, Callum was looking through the living room.

"Anything?" I asked him.

"Fuck it, let's break in," Callum said. I was with him; we

could easily repair that shit later. We should have done that in the first place. We could easily laugh about it later if it was just a misunderstanding.

Mateo looked up at us, his face blanched of color.

"Wait," he hissed.

He threw the phone at Callum and me.

Callum took the phone and pressed Play where Mateo had left the recording. He came to stand behind us, and we began to watch.

There were no cameras inside, but we had them surrounding the house and the yard. The video showed footage of the person who was driving the car. They drove recklessly down into our territory.

They then parked and turned off the light. As if the person knew they would be watched, they had their whole face covered.

"We need to go in right now," I pleaded.

"Not yet," Cal managed to say. I knew him, and saying that had cost him. "We walk inside not knowing who's there..." because now we were sure someone was, "We'll put her in more danger."

Fuck.

He was right.

I hated what they were saying, but it was the only way.

"She's tough. And it won't be long now," Mateo told me, but his look said otherwise. This was killing all of us.

So we watched the recording. We were switching between angles. The seconds ticked by, and I was coming out of my fucking skin.

We wanted to keep our girl safe, but everyone kept coming at us at every angle.

"Go back," I said.

It was a camera angled between the side of the house

and the front. The man could be seen, and he turned his head for a fraction, but it was enough for me to recognize him.

You didn't spend an hour holding on to someone's bloody wound without remembering everything about them.

"The mayor," I whispered.

29

MATEO

Everyone took life for granted, thinking tomorrow was already promised, when that couldn't be further from the truth. Our days were borrowed. We all had a death day. We just didn't know when it was coming.

I was praying to God that today was not one of ours. It couldn't be. It wasn't possible for people to eat shit all their lives without at least basking in paradise—and we had barely gotten a taste of it.

Life was a fucking bitch.

Everly was the first good thing we had in a long time.

"We need to get it together," Cal said, pulling it together faster than us.

Saint still looked like he wanted to break in already. We all did, but it would put us all in more danger if the mayor had a gun. For him to come here, he had to be erratic already, and those people were the most dangerous ones.

"I bet he took her into the garage," I said.

"I agree, or else Saint would have seen them when he did a sweep."

"How the hell did he get in there so fast?" Saint asked. "We were out in seconds."

That was what I was trying to figure out.

Callum was thinking about it when he looked up at us. "He was already in."

Both Saint and I looked at him, confused.

"The window," he said like it explained everything. "She didn't see him outside, he was already in—she just saw a reflection."

"And the fucker probably ran and hid in the bathroom while we ran around like headless fucking chickens."

Fucking shit.

"And we told her to lock herself in," Saint hissed.

Even if she wanted to run, it would have taken more time to unlock the door.

"My room is on the far end, let's go through there."

As Cal and I got to work on my window, Saint was out getting a few things we told him to get.

"Not a sound," Cal reminded us as he jumped in.

I jumped in after Callum, and then Saint handed us each a metal pipe. I pulled my phone out and sent one text message.

"Let's do this," I told them.

We walked slowly to make sure the old floors didn't warn the mayor we were coming. A man like him wouldn't want to kill Everly right away. He wasn't a killer, and he was desperate. He wanted to hurt her, but he was still in bed with her uncle. The mayor was a lot of things, but a killer wasn't one of them. So we banked on the fact that it wouldn't be his first thing on the list.

When we got to the kitchen, beads of sweat were starting to drip down my forehead. It was killing me to not fucking run in there and I knew it was killing my brothers too. I went ahead to one side of the door, and Callum took the other side.

We signaled to three and then tried to open the door, but it was fucking locked.

Son of a bitch.

He was counting on us to come, wasn't he?

Saint silently backed away, probably to get something to open the door.

Both Cal and I put our ears to the door, trying to see if we could hear something.

"Ruined everything! No one was poking around."

The mayor's voice sounded unhinged.

"Except for David, right?"

Relief coursed through me at the sound of our girl's voice. I saw Cal take a relieved breath.

"I'm going to take care of all of you like we did with Dave."

We always knew they had something to do with the old man's death, but hearing him saying it sent a blind rage through me. My hand moved on its own, but Callum gripped me by the wrist.

When we looked at one another, we knew that the mayor wasn't coming out of this alive.

He touched our girl, and worst of all, he helped kill the only father figure we had ever known.

Saint came back and handed me two metal pins.

Callum whispered into his ear as I began to work the lock.

"I said shut up, you little bitch!"

The mayor's roar could be heard by all of us. We needed to be quick because he was at his tipping point.

I felt the little click that meant the lock was undone. I turned to my brothers, and we busted inside. The first thing I noticed was Everly tied up and sitting on a chair. But that wasn't where my eyes went to. It was to the mayor who was standing in front of her, one hand still in the air while Everly's face was turned.

"Motherfucker," Saint hissed.

The mayor turned to us, and that was when we noticed the gun. He raised it with a shaky hand. The look on his face was mad. This was nothing like the man who paraded around this town.

Saint didn't hesitate—he was in a blind rage, going straight for the mayor's kneecaps. I ran to the mayor and used the opportunity to get the firearm away from him. Guns were dangerous in the hands of those who didn't know how to use them.

Callum ran to Everly while we neutralized the situation.

There was murder in his eyes too.

"Don't kill him," he reminded Saint.

The mayor thrashed around, and I used the opportunity to throw the gun away from us before he could pull the trigger. Once the loud thud of it could be heard, Saint backed off while I took the mayor and wrapped an arm around his neck.

"Go to sleep, fucker," Saint seethed as the mayor lost consciousness.

I turned to look at Everly. Callum had her in his arms. Her cheek was a little red but otherwise okay. She looked shaken up but that was expected.

"You okay, mamas?" I asked as I laid the mayor on the floor.

Everly nodded as her eyes went to the mayor. "He was in the house the whole time," she said.

"Yeah," Cal said as he kissed the top of her head.

"He watched us," she added slowly, and the three of us just looked at each other.

Saint went to Everly next, switching places with Cal, while he brought me the ropes that the asshole had used to tie Everly with.

"We made it so easy for him, didn't we?" I said aloud.

Anything he could have wanted was at his fingertips here.

"Don't," Everly's soft voice scolded me. I looked up at her and gave her a forced smile. "We couldn't have known he was going to do that."

She was right, but it still got to me, and I knew it got to my brothers too. I was glad it was the three of us who protected her.

"What happened?" Saint asked her.

Everly began to recap what we already suspected. He had taken her from the room. She tried to get away, but he caught her. He pointed the gun at her to threaten her not to move. Then he tied her up.

"He said nothing was going to plan anymore, and that it was all your fault."

Yeah, because he saw us with Lorenzo, he blamed us. The rope around his neck got tighter because he was a puppet for two men.

"What else?" This time I asked the question.

"He said that it was my fault... for being a whore."

My nostrils flared, Cal's jaw went rigid, and Saint's eyes darkened.

"Keep going," Cal told her.

The air in the room had gone electric with rage.

"He admitted to killing Dave." She whispered that part, but we all heard it.

"Can you walk?" I asked her.

She looked at Callum, then at me, and lastly up at Saint.

"I'm fine," she said. "I knew you guys would come for me."

This girl—there was no one like her.

"Go with Saint," I said as I began to lift the mayor.

"What are you guys going to do?" she questioned us.

"Saint," Callum began to say as he helped me with the mayor. "Turn off all the lights. Then go with Everly and start it up."

They didn't ask any more questions as they left.

"What did Lorenzo say?" Cal asked me.

I balanced the mayor on one hand and then reached for my phone.

"No blowback." I grinned at him.

30

CALLUM

When Everly and Saint had disappeared, I shouldered more of the mayor's weight while Mateo called Lorenzo.

"No answer," he muttered after a while, jabbing at his phone with a frown on his face.

"Leave him a message. Tell him it's urgent. Try calling him back later. In the meantime, we've got an interrogation to do."

We dragged the mayor outside to where the crane waited next to the crusher, turned on by Saint and Everly. Everly gave us a small wave from her position on Saint's lap which made me smile, even in the middle of this shit we'd been dragged into.

"Are you thinking what I'm thinking?" Mateo's gaze went to one of the bear traps that was stacked on its side next to some tires.

"Bear trap first, then the car?" I scanned the rows of twisted metal machines, until my gaze hit on one. It was a small blue Mini. The whole top of it had been ripped off in a collision with a huge rig, and it was perfect for our purposes. We'd already stripped it of anything useful, and all that remained was the bare bones of the vehicle, and the passenger seat, which had been unsalvageable. "The Mini?"

"Bear trap in the car," Mateo decided. "Tie him to the seat, put the bear trap at his feet, when he panics—*snap*."

He looked disturbingly excited by the idea, but I just shook my head with a small smile. Whatever we did to the mayor tonight wouldn't be enough payback for all the innocent lives he'd taken. He had blood on his hands, and now we would too, but the difference was, we were doling out justice. "Okay. Help me get everything into position."

I called up to Saint to let him know which car we wanted, and he nodded, helping Everly maneuver the swinging crane arm until it was positioned over the Mini. I watched as the claw lowered, still keeping a tight grip on the mayor in case he woke up and decided to do something stupid.

The claw easily picked up the remains of the small car, and Saint and Everly carefully swung the crane arm around, then began to lower the car until it was right in front of us. As soon as the claw released its grip, Mateo and I began dragging the mayor over to the car. The doors had been pulled off, which made our job easier, and soon we had him on the wrecked passenger seat.

"Ropes or chains?" I turned to Mateo.

Before he could reply, a long, thin chain landed next to me, pooling on the dirty ground. From the crane's cab, Saint saluted me, and I gave him a nod.

"These chains work. They're thin, but easily strong enough to hold him. Get the bear trap while I tie him up."

We worked quickly, Mateo returning with the bear trap and carefully positioning it in the footwell before setting it. As I finished tying the mayor up, he started coming to with a groan. Quickly hitting the audio record function on my phone, I placed it on the stack of tires next to the car, where it would easily pick up the conversation.

Now it was time to begin.

"You have good timing," I told him as his eyes blinked open.

"Let me go!" He immediately began to struggle against the chains.

"I wouldn't do that if I were you." Mateo stepped up to the car, pointing down into the footwell. "Not unless you want your leg snapped off."

He recoiled, his face going an interesting pallid green shade. Yeah, now the fucker realized just how much trouble he was in.

Casually folding my arms across my chest, I stared at him. "We have questions. If you answer them to our satisfaction, we'll think about letting you go. You refuse, or you don't give us the answers we want, then that bear trap will be the least of your worries."

Of course, he didn't know that we had no intention of letting him go.

"If you don't let me go, there'll be hell to pay. You don't know what you're getting yourselves involved in."

Quick as lightning, Mateo rounded the side of the car and backhanded him across the face. "Wrong answer." He smiled. "How did that feel? You did it to Everly."

The mayor spat at Mateo, who aimed a punch at his stomach. He jerked, scrambling to hold his legs away from the trap. Turning a murderous look on me, he bared his teeth. "Fuck you. Fine. What are your questions?"

"First question. You admitted to killing Dave. I want to hear the full story from your mouth."

If he cooperated, this was going to be hard to listen to,

and that was why I wanted Saint and Everly out of the way. Sure, they'd hear his confession afterward when we listened to the audio recording, but this way, we could hopefully soften the blow first.

"Dave? The owner of this piece-of-shit boneyard? I can't take all the credit for that. Little Everly Walker's dear old uncle put the fear of God in him, gave him a heart attack in his office, didn't he? The dumb old man took the information he had on us straight to Mr. Walker. If I'd been there, we could've played it off; the man had nothing solid he could pin on us, but no, the dean decided that he'd scare the man into a heart attack." The words were spat out bitterly, and Mateo and I exchanged glances. There was obviously a rift in their relationship, probably had been since the mayor had been shot, if I had to guess.

"So what did you do?"

"Mr. Walker thought he was too good to get his hands dirty. I had to finish off the job. It was easy enough—I just force-fed him a few pills, enough to finish the job the heart attack started. Nice and simple."

Both Mateo and I were seething, and I wanted this fucker to die, but we needed the rest of the answers.

"What information did he have on you?"

The mayor shot me a knowing look. "I'm not dumb, boy. I know that you know exactly what that information was."

I exhaled heavily, keeping my voice calm with an effort. "Okay, next question. Tell us what happened to Dave's son. Tell us what happened to Erick."

31

MATEO

The amount of self-control we were executing right now was something I didn't think would have been possible before Everly. Our goal had been getting revenge at whatever cost, and deep down, I think we knew that cost might be bloody.

It wasn't going to be anymore, and now we had more to fight for.

"Okay, next question. Tell us what happened to Dave's son. Tell us what happened to Erick."

Callum's question was the one we had been asking ourselves since we were little boys. Erick's disappearance and death had set a catalyst for us. We were who we were today because of that.

My heart was pounding faster as I waited for the fucker's response.

Hearing how he killed Dave was something we had already guessed at. So his confession still hurt, but it wasn't new. We now prepared ourselves because when it came to Erick and all we'd discovered, it was bound to fucking kill.

That was why we didn't want Everly or Saint there. They

were strong, but some things stuck with you until the day you died, and this was not going to be one of those things for them.

The mayor started to fidget, as if that would make him get loose from his chains. It almost made me grin.

I got closer and bent down so we were at eye level.

"It's in your best interests to answer the questions," I told him. "You don't need all ten fingers—or your balls—to live."

His eyes widened. He looked from me to Callum until he decided that talking was in his best interest. He was probably thinking of all the ways he would get us afterward.

Someone like the mayor didn't go missing just like that without repercussions. There was a security blanket that came with the title. Unlucky for him, Lorenzo did not care for that blanket, and lucky for us, our goals aligned.

"Who gives a shit about orphanage boys?" the mayor spat at us.

At this point, I was sure he wanted to goad us into doing something reckless.

"All they do is take money away from the state. The fewer of you lowlifes there are, the better. You're nothing but a waste of space, draining government resources."

We were fucking fuming now.

This was complete bullshit.

Callum gripped the good ol' mayor by the throat until he was wheezing, gasping for air.

"Answer the fucking question," he proceeded to say.

"Everything okay?" Saint's voice was getting closer.

"Yeah," I called out. "Take care of Everly."

He nodded and sent us a salute, and then went back. He wouldn't be happy with us for keeping him from the action, but he was the one that took Erick's disappearance the hardest.

"Let him go, Cal, before he faints."

Callum stepped back, and that's when the smell hit us both.

"He fucking peed," I said disgustedly.

"You can't treat me like this!" the mayor spat, still thinking he had some leverage over us.

My hand went to his jaw, gripping him and forcing him to look up at us. I knew he could feel the indents of my fingertips trying to claw their way into his skin.

"If you talk, we can help you deal with the dean," I lied. "You're the mayor. The town needs you, but someone like him—a dean? He can be replaced."

I swear to God, his eyes looked like they sparkled with temptation.

"Now, talk," Callum demanded one last time.

Cal and I stood side by side, our arms crossed, hoping that we were done with the bullshit.

The mayor licked his lips. "It used to be easier taking boys from the foster homes. No one gave a shit about them..." he began to say as I held my breath. "That was the chief's idea. He knew better about how that system worked. I pulled a few strings; no one realized they went missing."

"Kinda like the dean targets students with no families," I spat.

The mayor's body shook as he laughed. "Ah, aren't statistics a great thing? The system sets them up for failure." He took a deep breath and went on. "They give those kids grants to go to school, and when they go missing, no one asks why, just another runaway, and no one cares because they have been in and out of the system their whole lives."

I looked at Cal, and I knew he was feeling the exact same way as me. I was going to ask more, but my phone rang and the call I was expecting came through.

"You got my message?" I asked.

Cal gave me a small smirk, knowing who was on the line.

"I'll be there soon," he said and then hung up.

"Okay, now tell us about Dave's son. Based on your records, after you took him, you stopped taking kids from the foster home," I said, trying to keep the conversation going. We needed to make this fast. Lorenzo would be here soon, and some things should stay family only.

"Ah, management changed, a do-gooder who wanted to change the world." He stopped talking and glared at us. "Then you three were sticking your noses everywhere. The chief had you on his radar ever since he found you guys lurking around in the dark asking questions."

"And why didn't you get us before?" Cal questioned him.

"You were just stupid kids, then that old bastard had to take you in. We thought the problem would have ended when he was taken care of."

My hands were shaking.

"What happened to the boy?" I seethed.

The mayor took a moment before answering, right before I was about to tell Callum to screw this and get it over with, if he was going to keep stalling.

"The chief found the boy wandering in the streets in the middle of the night. He said he had seen him with a woman earlier, and their altercation caught his attention. He stuck around and then offered the boy a ride home. When he found out he was in the system, he ran a check on him."

Callum closed his eyes as if he realized something I didn't.

"Blood like his is precious. He was a little gold mine," the mayor finished saying.

Then it hit me. The blood type that was listed on his file. The universal donor one.

"You motherfucker," I spat, trying to get a step forward, but Cal put out a hand to stop me.

Cal then went up to the mayor and put his hands on either side of his face.

"Thank you," he said in a low, lethal voice. "We won't be able to do the same thing you did with Erick, but I think we'll get fucking close."

Callum sent Saint the signal and the machine started to run.

He then stepped away as the mayor started to look around in panic.

"See you in hell," I spat at him.

32

CALLUM

It was time. The mayor was shouting, looking around him desperately, but none of us cared.

My gaze went to Everly, still perched on Saint's lap inside the crane. She shouldn't have to see this.

I signaled to Saint, who gave me a nod. He opened the door of the crane cab, lifting Everly out, and followed after her.

When they were on the ground, Everly raised her chin, determination in her eyes. "I know he's going to die, and I want to see."

The three of us exchanged glances. We wanted to protect our girl.

She seemed to read our minds, shaking her head angrily. "No. You are *not* leaving me out. I'm just as involved as you are. I want justice, just like you do."

Fuck. She was right, but none of us wanted her to see this. I didn't even want Saint to see it, but going by the expression on his face, he wouldn't stand aside.

"You stay over there." I pointed to the stacks of cars to our left. At least if she was there, she wouldn't have a clear view of what we were going to do, although she would know what was happening.

She glanced toward the stacks, then back again, and when I widened my eyes, giving a pointed look in Saint's direction, she nodded.

"Saint? I don't want to be alone."

The shiver that went through her was completely genuine, and I knew then that keeping her away had been the best idea. Our girl was strong—very fucking strong—but this... this was enough to turn the stomach of the most hardened person. I was counting on Saint to protect her from the worst of it, which would in turn protect him.

The second they'd moved into position, I gave a nod to Mateo, who grinned widely, heading for the crane. The whole time, the mayor had been struggling and shouting threats, but we'd all ignored him. Better that he tired himself out.

I moved around the car, stepping right up to him.

"Look at you now. The mayor of Blackstone. You thought you were untouchable. Did you know that your wife had a coke habit, and was fucking anyone she could behind your back? Did you know about your son's coke habit too? You fucked him up for life, that's for sure."

He glared at me, and something in his eyes made me realize.

"You knew, didn't you? You knew how you were fucking up your family, and you didn't even care."

His lip curled. "Foolish boy. You know nothing about the real world."

I almost laughed at his false bravado, but I held my composure. Instead, I leaned into him, speaking into his ear. "Do you know why they call this the boneyard?"

I waited to hear his sharp intake of breath, his whole

body beginning to shake as he finally accepted the fact that he wasn't getting out of here alive.

Softly, I spoke the final words that would seal his fate.

"You're about to find out."

Then I raised my hand in the air and stepped back.

While I'd been talking, Mateo had lowered the claw so it was almost touching the car. Now, he closed the remaining distance, and as soon as the arms of the claw closed around the Mini, I took another step back, giving Mateo a thumbs up.

The crane began to lift the car into the air, and the scream that came from the mayor was almost inhuman. I remained impassive, watching as Mateo let the car swing for a moment before steadying the crane arm.

The mayor's movements became more frantic as he desperately tried to free himself, and I held my breath, knowing what was coming.

The cry of agony that filled the boneyard was accompanied by a loud *snap*, as the bear trap sprung. I winced, bile rising in my throat.

"Oh, snap," Saint muttered, giving me a grin even as he held Everly to him, her body curled into his and his hands covering her ears.

The screaming wouldn't stop. We had to hurry. Even with our position with the people of the south side, screams coming from the junkyard in the early hours of the morning wouldn't go unnoticed.

Mateo seemed to recognize the urgency, because the crane rose at three times the speed it had before.

When it was positioned above the car crusher, the machine on, the lethal metal jaws already churning, ready to chew whatever we dropped into a million pieces, I took a deep breath.

"This is for Dave and for Erick!" My shout echoed around the junkyard.

"And for all those innocent victims!" Everly's voice joined mine, and we all turned to look at her. She'd pulled away from Saint, and she was standing with her shoulders back, her hair blowing in the night breeze. Her eyes glittered, vengeance written all over her face, and I knew right then that we'd underestimated her.

She wasn't someone to be protected. She was our motherfucking queen.

We all ignored the increasingly hoarse screams of the mayor, our eyes meeting, reinforcing our connection. The Boneyard Kings and their queen. No one could tear us apart. Together, we were unstoppable.

Mateo lowered the crane arm, so it was just above the crusher. I moved to stand with Saint and Everly.

"Are you ready for this? Look away if you need to."

Saint shook his head, gripping my bicep. "No, brother. I'm with you."

Everly slipped her hand into mine. "He destroyed the lives of too many innocent people. He needs to pay."

Mateo was watching us, a question in his eyes, and I gave him a small nod.

I saw him put his finger over the button.

The crane's arms opened, releasing the Mini with the mayor inside.

It dropped straight into the crusher.

The harsh sound of metal on metal, combined with the mayor's screaming, reverberated around the junkyard.

Then I heard the crunch of human bones being crushed into pieces, and it was something I knew I'd never forget.

33

SAINT

A part of me felt like crying. It was like the emotions I felt inside of me were too much to contain. Anger was the main one, but also relief. I held on to Everly a little tighter as the three of us watched the mayor die.

We were no strangers to death. Hell, that bitch had been chasing us since the day we were born. All four of us had mourned the death of someone we loved. But now this was different; no one was taken from us, but instead, we took.

There was something to be said about taking justice into your own hands. Judging someone for their sins and giving them their execution was liberating.

The three of us turned when he heard Mateo's footsteps crunching through the dark.

It was over—for now.

One down, and two more to go.

Everly was holding on to Cal's hand. I let her go and just held on to her other hand, trying to feel her warmth. There was nothing like death to make you feel cold.

Mateo was probably seeking that same warmth Callum and I were tightly grasping.

He just looked up ahead to where he had essentially delivered the killing blow. He came up behind Everly and wrapped his arms around her waist, then placed his head in the crook of her neck, hiding his face in her hair.

His mother was a devout Catholic woman, and now he had stained his soul protecting those he loved. We all had. Because we were in this together.

We stayed like that in a chain for a few minutes, when Mateo's phone pinged with a message.

Lorenzo was here.

Mateo kissed Everly on the cheek and then pulled away.

Ideally, we wouldn't want Everly anywhere near Lorenzo. The less he knew of her, the better. He was the type of man who would use anything and anyone to get his way —and Everly was nobody's bargaining chip.

But after what had just happened, we didn't want to be apart.

"I'm not going anywhere," our beautiful girl stated.

The three of us gave her amused looks.

"Stay close to us, mamas," Matty told her.

"Try not to speak too much," I told her.

She gave me a look and was probably going to bitch me about, but Callum interfered.

"Lorenzo is not a friend,"he reminded us all.

I gave Everly a quick hug and then kissed her forehead.

Could we go back to earlier? When I was eating her out and her pussy was grinding against my face? Because that had been fantastic.

Today I learned that nothing killed a post-orgasmic glow faster than murder.

This time, I let Everly go with Callum. He needed her right now. I knew those two wanted to protect us, but we didn't need them to. With them at our backs, there was no reason to fear anything.

I walked a few steps in front of them with Mateo.

"How are you feeling?" I asked him.

"I'm fine, Saint, just fucking tired."

"Yeah, I could have used more beauty sleep," I said, and Callum and Everly laughed. I turned to look back at them. "Everly will not tell you this because she probably thinks your dark circles look hot or some shit, but they aren't."

"There's something seriously wrong with you," Cal joked.

"It's all that crack his mama did, we know this," Mateo added, and laughed.

"Well, if you're scared, I can tell you a bedtime story, Matty," I joked, and he rolled his eyes at me.

"I've had enough of your stories," he said, as we saw the blinding lights coming from the other side of the gate.

"And then we can buy a huge house, with a pool," I told them as I stared up at the ceiling. It was late, but I had gotten in a bit ago. When Tiff needed an out, she didn't care what time it was. They were all up because of me.

Every kid I knew hated the foster home, but I loved coming here. It was better than staying at home. I had friends here that felt more like family than my own mother.

"You don't even know how to swim," Erick mocked me.

"Yeah, no one is giving you mouth-to-mouth," Mateo added.

"Cal, you'll save me, right?" I asked in the direction of his bunk bed.

I heard his sigh. "Saint, more bullshit comes out of your mouth than your ass, there's no way I'll help you."

"You don't see me in weeks, and this is the thanks I get?" I was a little hurt.

"Fine we can have a pool," Cal was the first to give in, and I smiled.

"Why a pool?" Mateo questioned.

"I don't know, seems like all rich people have one. Hell, maybe I'll learn how to swim."

I heard their chuckles, and it brought a smile to my face.

"Saint..." Erick began to say. "We'll make your mom go away."

Erick had sounded so confident back then, that I'd almost believed him. We didn't have a big house or a pool, but we had more than a lot of rich people did. We had a brotherhood, we had love, and that was more than enough.

"We'll wait here," Cal said, and we nodded because that was best.

Mateo and I ran up ahead to unlock the gate. We each opened one of the sides and as soon as we did, two of Lorenzo's cars made their way inside. As soon as they got in, we closed it behind them.

Both Mateo and I looked across the street where the mayor had left his car, and knew we needed to get rid of it fast. That was going to be our next task after Lorenzo.

No way in hell were we splitting up right now.

Mateo and I ran back just as Lorenzo and Rigo were getting out of the car.

"*Compas*," Rigo greeted us. Right now, I didn't have time for his excitement. Still, we all nodded.

I stood next to Cal, while Mateo went to the other side of Everly. We could see the way they looked at her with curious eyes.

"Long night, eh?" Lorenzo smirked at us.

"You could say that," Mateo said.

Yeah, this was not the time to beat around the bush. I was tired, and I just wanted to go to bed and put this day behind us.

I looked at Lorenzo and when our gazes locked, I spoke.

"We killed the mayor."

34

EVERLY

The sky was beginning to lighten as the man stood in front of us, and I took a good look.

So this was Lorenzo.

My eyes scanned him. Tall, dark hair, dark eyes, muscular, he was an incredibly good-looking man, in a hard, dangerous way—if that made any sense—but I only had eyes for my three kings.

Ignoring Saint's words for a moment, he quirked a brow at Callum. "I was beginning to think you'd made her up." Callum just rolled his eyes, and then Lorenzo's attention turned to me. "Everly Walker? You're even more beautiful than they said."

I couldn't help smiling—not once had anyone mentioned that this guy had charm. I suppose it made sense when I thought about it, though. You didn't get to be in his position without charisma. And I guess the stories about him didn't hurt either.

He spoke with words like honey, but underneath, I knew there was a man who wouldn't hesitate to slit your throat if you crossed him.

When he turned away from me, Mateo curled his arm around my waist, and placed a light kiss on my cheek. Lorenzo conferred with the guy who he'd come with, and then gave a short nod.

"So, the mayor is dead. How did it happen?"

Saint gave him a quick rundown of the situation, with Callum and Mateo interjecting. The picture they painted wasn't a good one. The mayor had deserved everything he had coming, and more.

By the end of the story, even Lorenzo was looking a little repulsed, although he managed to keep his expression mostly neutral. "I'll see to it that it's covered up. There won't be any blowback. Usually, you'd owe me, but this time, I'd say you acted in the best interests of everyone on the south side." He hesitated for a moment, then added, "If you need any help taking care of your little problem with the dean or the police chief, it would be my pleasure to assist."

His eyes glimmered with malice as he smiled, and a shiver went down my spine. I was just glad he was on our side.

Callum stepped up and shook Lorenzo's hand. "We appreciate it."

He gave a short nod. "Back to business. I need the rest of the merch."

Callum and Mateo disappeared into the stacks with him and his man, and Saint came over to me, pulling me into his arms. "How are you feeling?"

Good question. How was I feeling?

I chewed on my lip. "Does it make me a bad person if I say I'm glad the mayor's dead?"

He laughed, kissing my head. "It doesn't make you a bad person. If it does, then I'm a bad person too, because I'm glad he's dead. One less scumbag in the world." Releasing me and taking my hand, he began pulling me across the yard. "Want to help me get rid of the rest of the evidence? We need to crush the car the mayor showed up in. Even the salvageable parts need to go—we can't risk leaving any of it behind."

"Okay."

The keys were long gone, but Saint used one of the tools from the workshop to get the doors open, then directed me to sit inside and steer while he pushed the car. Together, we managed to roll it over to where the crusher was located, and then he took my hand, pulling me out.

"Back in the crane."

"Again." I settled myself on his lap, and together, we effortlessly worked the controls, lifting the car into the air, and then positioning it over the crusher. It dropped inside, and the grinding sound started up. I knew that noise would forever remind me of what had happened to the mayor. I had blood on my hands now, but I knew that it had been deserved.

Once business was taken care of and Lorenzo had left, there was only an hour until classes began. Mateo drove my Camaro, following Callum as he drove the truck. Somehow, we made it to the campus on time, and after Callum came to a stop in the student parking lot, and Mateo joined us after parking my car, Saint handed us all energy drinks.

"I figured we could all use these to make it through the day."

I gratefully popped the top off mine, taking a large gulp. I'd only had a few hours' sleep—none of us had had more than that, in fact. Saint had a swim meet today, Callum and I had chess club, and Mateo had an engine tune-up booked in once his classes finished. We still had to keep the junkyard running as normal, fit in our schoolwork so we could get our degrees, and find a way to take down the two remaining most powerful men in Blackstone, before they figured out that we'd been the one to take down the mayor.

I had to have faith we'd accomplish it.

As we exited the parking lot, Saint froze. "Fuck," he muttered, glancing over to the left, and I followed his gaze. Robbie was leaning against one of the buildings, surrounded by some of his jock friends and their usual crowd of girls. "I'm betting he doesn't know what's happened to the mayor yet, but when he does find out, it's not gonna be easy being in the frat house."

"He won't suspect anything," Callum reassured him. "No one will suspect anything. The only cameras in that area are the ones we control, and I'm heading back after my morning classes to erase the footage."

Callum's words seemed to help, because his face became a little brighter, and then he broke out his flirtatious grin, turning it on me. "Everrrly. Wanna come and watch me swim today?"

Tilting my head, I raised a brow. "Is that even a question?" Because a chance to watch one of my guys, soaking wet in tiny Speedos? I was not going to pass that up.

"I'll see you later for chess club, baby. I need to get to my class now." Callum leaned down and pressed a kiss to my cheek, then after saying goodbye to Mateo and Saint, he sauntered off, seemingly unaware of the appreciative glances he was receiving as he walked away. My stomach flipped, watching him, and I wondered for the hundredth time how I'd managed to get so lucky, to be able to call these three insanely hot guys mine.

"I've got class too. Be at my swim meet on time." Saint placed a loud, smacking kiss on my lips, gave my ass a squeeze, then did the same to Mateo's ass, making him shout and swing at Saint. Saint just laughed, flipping him off as he walked backward away from us.

Mateo returned the gesture, but he was biting back a grin. When he looked at me, he let it free, giving me a wide smile. He took my hand in his. "Come on. I'll walk you to class."

35

MATEO

We were all so fucking tired. My head was starting to pound, making it hard to focus on my classes. I was sure that out of all of us, I struggled the most with school shit. That was why by the time the final bell rang, I was glad to go home.

Saint had his swim stuff, and Cal and Everly had their chess. Hopefully, not a lot of people would come to the yard today. Not that I minded, but I didn't like to work on cars while I was tired.

I took the truck and left them the Camaro.

We had killed the mayor, and this shit still felt surreal. Life was fragile, right? It was easy to end a life once you were determined enough. We cleaned up the blood. I didn't think people knew just how much blood there was in the human body. After that was done, we had to scrap the car the mayor had driven to our house.

Now the question was, how long until they reported him missing?

On the way home, I made a last-minute decision and stopped by the town hall. The guys would probably get mad that I'd come here on my own, but no one suspected us, and stopping by for permit work was nothing we hadn't done before.

The place didn't seem out of the ordinary. Everything seemed to be normal, especially for us looking within, but I wondered how freaked out those working in the office were, now that their beloved mayor had gone into radio silence?

I walked inside and made my way to the receptionist.

"How may I help you?" she asked, without looking up at me.

"I was looking to get a permit to update the fencing on our property," I said.

"What's the property?" she asked, still not looking up, but I knew that would change as soon as I rattled off the address.

And it had her head snapping my way instantly. "Oh, for the yard?"

I smiled at her and nodded.

She looked at me and then tilted her head back. "Oh, that's for a commercial license. It's different for residential, so you'll have to come back tomorrow since the person in charge isn't here."

Not that I was surprised. I was sure the mayor would have wanted to handle our request but now that he wasn't here, she had to stall.

"No problem, I'll stop again soon."

I walked out, but through the reflection of the window, I saw her pick up the phone and make a call.

Once I made it home, I made sure everything was locked up and just opened the garage so I could hopefully do the one job and then nap. I was waiting for my appointment to show up when the last person I ever thought would set foot in here did.

I almost wished she would have come last night, two birds with one stone kind of thing.

"Can I help you?" I bit out while I glared at her.

Tiff rolled her eyes and curled her lip in disgust. Putting her side by side with Saint, it was hard to see how they were related.

All her drug addiction had made her skin wrinkled and dry. She looked older than she was. Her hair was dull and dead. Still, you had to give it to the bitch, she still walked in like she was the shit. Someone needed to tell her she was nothing but a corpse.

"I'm here to see my baby," she said in her hoarse-ass voice.

"He don't wanna see you," I said as I continued to glare at her.

She ignored this and pulled out a cigarette and lighter from her bra. For a chain smoker, she sure as shit had been lucky not to get sick.

"My baby always wanna see me," she gloated.

My blood was boiling now, but I knew I couldn't do anything. If I so much as spooked her, she would run to the police and would say I hit her, and things were tense enough they would take her story and run with it.

"Doesn't your word mean shit?" I asked her. "Didn't the old man pay you off? Why are you dead set on hitting up Saint, if you know deep down he fucking hates you?"

I could tell she didn't like what I had to say.

Her beady little eyes looked around the garage, probably thinking of how much money she could make of all the tools we had. I wouldn't doubt if she was making a mental note to ask one of her dipshit lovers to help her.

"We have cameras everywhere, Tiff. A screw goes missing, and we come after you."

She did one last sweep, then her eyes landed on me.

"I want to see my baby. He isn't returning my texts, so tell him I won't leave until he talks to me."

This was news to me. We barely gave her cash, but the bitch probably wanted more—she always did.

Having had enough, I stood up and walked closer to her. She took a step back, and that made me grin.

"He's not here. So, leave and forget about him," I said in a lethal tone.

Being the dumb bitch she was, she wasn't going to heed the warning.

"All you little assholes have always been a pain in my ass. Telling me what I can or cannot do with my baby."

She was talking out of her ass because Callum and I had tried to stay away from their drama out of respect for Saint.

"Get out of my property before I call the cops for trespassing," I lied.

They would be the last people we would call, but she didn't need to know this.

She walked out, and a black car picked her up. Nicer than the cars her boyfriends usually had. I was trying to see who her new lover was, but the windows were too tinted to see.

Once she was gone, I could feel a headache starting to form. I pulled out my phone and called Cal.

"What happened?" he asked, on high alert.

"Nothing bad," I said right away, reassuring him. "Tiff paid a visit."

He stayed quiet because it had been a long time since she had come.

"Did you tell Saint?"

"Not yet, I don't think we should. It's not like she's expecting us to."

I hated to lie to him, but he needed to let the bitch go.

"We'll talk about it later; his meet will be soon."

Once Cal hung up, our client finally showed up. Once I started to work on the car, my problems started to fade.

Whatever came our way, we would handle it together, and that made it all bearable.

36

EVERLY

Hallie and Mia both came with me to watch Saint's swim meet. I'd say it was partly about the fact that the three of us hadn't hung out for a while, and partly because there were hot men to drool over.

Except, five minutes into the meet, after Saint had strutted out of the locker room in all his half-naked glory and blown me a kiss before executing a perfect dive into the pool, it became clear that neither of those reasons were true.

They'd chosen to sit on either side of me, and they exchanged glances before leaning closer. Mia was the first to speak. "Everly. We thought you should know..." She paused, taking a deep breath, then continued, "There are rumors going around about you."

My eyes widened. "Rumors? What rumors?"

She screwed up her face. "Ugh. I don't even wanna say. Okay, I'm just going to say it. The girls in my sorority are saying that you're sleeping with all three of the Boneyard Kings. They're calling you awful names, Ev, saying you're a slut and a ho and other things I can't even bring myself to repeat."

Hallie added, "Even the guys are talking about it, and it's not just the Boneyard Kings. Jon said you were dating Robbie, then you cheated on him with the kings, and then you slept with him again and gave him an STD."

I stared at her, open-mouthed. "What? I can't—Who? Who said I was with Robbie and cheated on him?"

Hallie pointed toward Jon, who was cutting through the water in the lane next to Saint. "Jon told me, and he said Robbie told him."

My jaw clenched.

"First of all, I told you that my relationship with Robbie was fake. I've never even kissed him, nor do I want to. Ever. I can't stand the guy."

A tiny trickle of guilt made its way through me at the thought that his father was now dead, and I'd had a hand in his death, but I reminded myself of the atrocious acts the mayor had committed and would have continued to commit.

"Hey, we believe you." Mia placed her hand on my knee. "Right, Hallie?"

Hallie was silent for a moment, and we both turned to look at her. I was taken aback by the bitter expression on her face. "I don't know, Everly. You said there was nothing going on with you and Saint, but that was a lie, wasn't it?"

"What do you mean?"

"I saw you with him at the ball!" Her voice rang out loudly, and she flushed, lowering it. "You were all over each other. If you lied about that, what else are you lying about?"

My stomach churned. "I promise you... I swear on my life, that I was never with Robbie. That was him making up a story, and yes, I went with it, but I never once even considered doing anything with him."

"What about the Boneyard Kings?" She folded her arms across her chest, her mouth set in a flat line.

I took a deep breath. Now my uncle knew that I was involved with them, there was no point trying to hide the truth anymore. And they'd openly kissed and hugged me this morning, right in the middle of the campus where anyone could see. "I'm with them. I... I'm in a relationship with the three of them."

Both girls inhaled sharply. "How does that work? Like, exclusive?" Mia's eyes were wide.

"Yeah. We're together, exclusively."

Hallie laughed without humor. "I'm sorry, but do you expect me to believe that one girl can keep the three hottest guys in this town satisfied? No offense, Everly, but I just don't see it. Even if you are with the three of them, they're probably all cheating on you."

I shook my head. They didn't understand—how could they? My relationship with my three guys was special. We had a deep connection that I knew people wouldn't get, looking in from the outside. I was completely secure in this relationship, and I knew they'd never cheat on me, just like I'd never cheat on them. We completed each other, as corny as it sounded.

"They're not cheating on me; they wouldn't do that. It's... it's hard to explain, but we have a connection. We're all committed to this relationship."

Mia shook her head, huffing out a soft laugh. "Wow. Okay. Well, I'm officially incredibly jealous of you right now." She squeezed my knee gently. "I'm happy for you, though. Like, I'm really jealous, but happy. If they make you happy, and you make them happy, then fuck what everyone else thinks. They don't get to have a say in your relationship."

"Thanks." I returned her smile, my shoulders slumping with relief.

Hallie remained silent for a while, her eyes narrowed as she thought. Eventually she said, "So tell us. Who has the biggest dick? Saint's rocking that big dick energy, but I have a feeling Mateo is just as big, if the rumors are true. And then Callum... mmm, that guy has a huge—"

"Hallie!" I hissed. "Please, stop talking!" People were beginning to look at us, and I could feel my face turning red.

In the best timing ever, I was saved by the coach's whistle blowing, and the swimmers began to climb out of the pool, to make room for the next lot who were preparing to dive in. I caught Saint's eye, and he was staring at me with a worried expression on his face.

I'm okay, I mouthed, and he nodded, shooting me a grin. Then he held up his hands in a heart shape. I couldn't stop my smile.

"He's really into you, isn't he?" Mia's voice was full of wonder. "I've never seen him look like that at any girl before."

As she said the words, and I held Saint's gaze, I realized that all three of the Boneyard Kings looked at me the way he was currently looking at me right now.

How did I get so lucky? I had a feeling I'd be asking myself the same question for a long time to come.

37

SAINT

My lungs hurt, my body was feeling weaker, and I knew I needed to breathe, but I refused to do it. I forgot how much I missed this type of exhaustion. The water was one of the first things to save me, to make me feel clean, like I wasn't a piece of shit and I deserved to keep on living.

I broke the surface with a gasp.

My heart rate was accelerating, and all my problems faded.

Since Everly had come into our lives, I had been spending less and less time at the frat house, but with what happened to the mayor, we figured I needed to be there to keep up appearances.

No one gossiped more than a bunch of little frat boys.

We needed to know what was going on with Robbie, specifically, what people were saying about the mayor's absence.

Swimming to the other end of the pool, I used my strength to pull myself out of the water. Once I was out, I took off my cap and goggles as I sat on the edge with my feet in the water. This year had felt like it had dragged at times, but at others, like it was going too fast, and I couldn't grasp it.

One thing I never feared was graduation, because I knew that no matter what happened after it was all over, I would still be with my brothers.

We always talked about our revenge and what would happen after justice for Erick was served, but we never really thought about the after that came with getting what you most wanted. The after was happening soon, and it was a melancholy feeling. I'd carried Erick with me for years, but it felt like the time to let him go, and finally rest, was getting near.

"What's something you want most in the world?" Erick asked me.

I sat up straighter, thinking about his question before answering with something stupid. Erick had a way of making you feel like you could touch the stars. He was wise in a different way than Cal.

"I guess I'd like Tiff to just leave me alone," I admitted. Which I felt guilty for saying since he also had a parent, but he had hopes of being reunited with his. If Tiff dropped me off here and never showed up again, I wouldn't be mad.

"That's all it'll take to make you happy?" he asked.

Before I could answer, Callum opened the door and ran in, with Mateo following behind and then closing the door.

"How did it go?" I asked, mostly because I didn't want to continue this conversation, because being with them here made me happy.

Cal and Mateo grinned at us, then pulled out the candy they'd gone to steal from the office and threw it at us.

"We're going to get busted for this tomorrow," Erick added with a disapproving nod, but still reached for a bar.

I looked at the water, letting it calm me, and even though so many things had changed, that one thing still remained the same.

I changed into my clothes, then I made my way to the frat house. As I pulled the door open, I almost felt like a fraud for being here. The brothers preached brotherhood, but they wouldn't hesitate to stab you in the back for their own gain. As kids, *my* brothers and I knew the meaning of that word. Good or bad. Ride or die. And we had been proving it over and over again.

As soon as I walked in, people stopped talking and stared. These were the guys I usually hung out with. No sign of Robbie and his crew yet.

"What, you've never seen someone so handsome before?" I joked, and a few chuckled.

"Where have you been, Devin?" someone asked.

"I heard he's pussy-whipped!" Someone else made a whooshing sound.

"What can I say, boys," I told them as I made my way to the stairs. "Saint Devin is a one-woman man!"

"Isn't she fucking those two other guys you hang with?"

My head turned to the person who said that, and my face became stony.

"You mean my brothers?"

They looked at each other, but no one said anything at first. Then one of the sophomores that I didn't mind spoke.

"It's kinda confusing to me since I come from a sheltered family, but hey, man, to each their own. I respect your sexual preference. I won't judge you."

Okay.

Then the guys kind of nodded among themselves.

And it dawned on me.

"Do you think I'm fucking my brothers?" I wanted to laugh, but then I didn't because at least they weren't judging.

"No offense, Devin, but the other way around."

I just stared at them and sighed. "And let me guess, you're all jealous you didn't confess your love for me," I joked.

"Fuck you, Devin," someone else yelled.

"You motherfuckers wish," I barked back. "No, we aren't fucking each other, and if anyone says anything disrespectful about my girl, I'll lay your ass out."

That's when a few of them looked uncomfortable.

"What?" I gritted out.

"There's a rumor that she gave Robbie an STD because of you guys."

That motherfucker.

"Where is Robbie?" I seized the opportunity to ask.

The guys looked at each other, then at me.

"You haven't heard?"

I shook my head, my throat going dry.

"He's been a mess lately. He went home because his dad hadn't come home in a few days."

"What do you mean?" I played stupid but it was the only way.

"They're going to file a missing person report. The chief is taking care of it all."

And there was another one of our problems.

Just then, the door opened, and I expected it to be Robbie, but it wasn't. Instead, it was one of his friends. He looked at me in disgust. "I told everyone that letting you into the frat was a bad idea. You're nothing but trash."

I took a step forward, but someone put a hand to my shoulder and stopped me. The guys I had just been talking to all turned to look at him, and a few of them stood in front of me. I didn't know if it was protectively or to stop me.

"Leave him alone," one of the guys broke out, and put a hand over his shoulder and dragged him to the game room.

And that was why I didn't like coming here anymore. I was ready to go up the stairs and lock myself in my room, when someone touched me. It was the sophomore.

"What's up?" I asked, since he looked like he wanted to tell me something.

"One of the girls that is always with your girlfriend has been spending a lot of nights with Robbie," he told me.

My jaw went hard.

That bitch.

If she didn't like me before, she was about to hate all of us.

38

MATEO

It was time for that one weekend of the month—time to open the shop for the people in our community. This time, everyone was up early. We knew Lorenzo had said no blowback, but after what Saint told us had gone down at the frat, we had all been on edge.

The other thing Saint had told us we had kept to ourselves. We didn't want to upset Everly just yet. I was all for taking care of the problem ourselves, but she wouldn't like that, and we just wanted to see if the rumors were true and if *she* was behind them. People were going to talk either way—people always did. It was easy to judge the things you didn't understand. Or because you were a jealous bitch, but the verdict was still up in the air on that one.

Now the three of us were sitting down, waiting for Saint to finish making breakfast.

Callum and Everly had Dave's old chessboard between them while they practiced for a meet.

"It smells so good," Everly moaned, and my dick perked to attention.

Callum's eyes darkened as he looked across the table at

her. Suddenly noticing our eyes on her, she glared and pointed a finger at us.

"Behave," she ordered.

"You could have been breakfast," Saint sighed as he flipped a pancake. "But you didn't want to."

She reached for a spoon and threw it at his butt.

Living with a woman was certainly something we weren't used to. It was all the soft things she did that unlocked memories about my mother I had buried inside. It was the way that she took care of us together and individually. She had a soft touch that was soothing all the jagged edges we were living with.

"I can't right now," she hissed at him as her cheeks turned pink.

"You can. You just don't want to." I leaned over and bit her cheek softly.

Callum licked his lips. "What they said."

Just then, Saint turned around and declared he was done. He brought forward a stack of pancakes on a plate, then another one with bacon, and the last had scrambled eggs.

Once that was on the table, he joined us. He turned to Everly and began to thrust his hips her way.

"A little blood on your sword is good for the soul, or so the saying goes," he deadpanned.

Everly started to laugh, and so did we. Who the hell knew where the fuck he was getting his sayings from, because they were something else.

"So, I was thinking, if we set up activities for the kids," Everly said, and we all just looked to see where she was going with this. She swallowed the bit of food she was chewing and kept going, "I noticed that a lot of people bring their kids when they come."

"Many of them don't have family or anyone they trust leaving their kids with," Cal told her.

She nodded.

I loved how understanding she was of it all, and she never judged.

"Yeah, I know. That's why if they're coming, we might as well make it fun for them. Buy some packs of juices to give them, and give their parents water or a soda."

My throat constricted, and from the silence of my brothers, I knew they felt the same way. This had been the legacy we had decided to take on our backs, and now she was making it her own.

I'd forever cherish the fact that she didn't run away from us.

"We can do that." Saint was the first to speak.

"Okay, let's finish eating because once the cars start, they won't stop until the sun goes down."

We all got changed and showered.

Cal and I usually went last since Everly and Saint liked to use all the hot water, and they took the longest to shower.

As I put my shit away, I noticed Cal was in the old man's room.

"I thought we'd clear it out tomorrow," he told me as he heard me come in.

"It's been long overdue," I said.

"Yeah," he added. "It just never felt right before."

"We should remodel the whole place, too," I said, looking around.

The house still looked the same as when we walked in here as boys.

"I was thinking of that too. Once I graduate, we can dedicate more time to the business and increase our revenue."

"Once we are out, we'll help you," I promised, knowing that the dean would soon stop being a problem.

We walked out of the room and went to the garage. It was already opened, and the sun was illuminating the room. Saint was getting all the tools ready while Everly set up a table with the drinks and snacks.

You took care of your community, and your community took care of you. And maybe we did it at first because it was what the old man taught us, but as we got older, who better than us to know how it felt to be cast aside and unwanted? It was why this side of town stuck together at times, because we were all outcasts.

The cars started to come, and each of us was hard at work. We were all sweating and tired by noon, but we knew that it was just one day out of the month, and we pulled through.

Everly's head turned to the long driveway when an old Beetle came our way. It used to be red, but it was all rusted. Now it looked orange. The windows were opened, and Eminem blasted from the old speakers.

Since the shorter lane now was Saint's, the car parked that way.

I could tell Everly didn't know whether to laugh or be scared when Esther got out of the car.

"Hi, babies," she greeted all of us, and then headed to the snack table where Everly was currently sitting.

"Oooh, sweetheart, now you know how to run a business," she said as she turned back and glared at us. "All this damn time, and these three dummies never offered me a drop of water."

The people around us chuckled, and so did we.

"You know they say a woman's touch changes things," Cal said since he was the closest to her.

"You got that right, boy."

I finished changing the oil on the car I was working on and was about to go inside and take a piss before starting another one, when everyone's heads turned toward the road, where we could hear police sirens getting louder.

Everly stood up, and Cal stopped working on the car and wiped his hands. Saint was standing next to Esther's car, and we all just watched as three cars pulled into our yard.

The people who were waiting in their cars locked their doors. They were scared. Everyone here knew that the police did nothing for them.

When I looked up again, I saw the chief of police, and I knew we were fucked. Cal and I looked at each other. They couldn't come in, not without a warrant. We began to walk to the front of the yard, but the chief wasn't even looking at us. He was making his way to Saint.

I opened my mouth to speak, but he beat me to it.

"Saint Devin," the asshole all but roared. "You are under arrest for the murder of Robert Parker-Pennington II."

39

EVERLY

Everything around me turned to chaos. People shouting, running around, freaking out. One minute, we'd been fine. Happy.

The next, *boom*.

It had all imploded with the arrival of the chief of police. I gritted my teeth as I looked at him, instinctively edging behind one of the cars that was parked close to me. I hadn't seen him since he and my uncle had taken me away, and the sudden flashbacks I was having were enough to send my heart rate skyrocketing.

"Are you okay?"

I turned to see Esther studying me, her brow creased, and I nodded. "I'm fine."

She gave me a skeptical look but didn't comment any further. Instead, she raised her hand, pointing in the direction of Saint. "Our boy needs to be saved."

"Yes. I'm not going to let him go, I promise." My words were breathless, full of fear, but she nodded, accepting them.

"I know you won't. You get my boy back, and you've got

free milkshakes for life." Giving me a wink, she ducked down to take a crying child into her arms. Her eyes flitted to mine again, and I nodded firmly. There was no way that I was letting the commissioner take Saint away. Not when I knew what he was capable of, and especially not now I knew that he held Saint responsible for the mayor's death.

There was no way he could've known what had happened to the mayor, so my guess was that Saint was a convenient scapegoat. If the mayor had gone rogue, this was a good way to tie up loose ends.

I was beyond glad that my uncle wasn't here. If he had been... I didn't even know how I'd have dealt with that.

An involuntary cry fell from my mouth when I saw Saint, cuffed and subdued, being led toward the gates where the cop car awaited. As they neared me, Saint's eyes went to the chief of police's, his gaze full of venom. "You fucking stupid—" His words were cut off by the police chief slamming his fist into his face.

A hush fell over the crowd.

Everyone's faces turned toward the police chief.

It was right then that I realized just how much of a community this was.

The rage that swelled within the crowd lifted me and gave me hope. It made me believe that we had people on our side. People who would fight for justice, to give those who were corrupt the punishment they deserved.

As Saint was unceremoniously shoved inside the cop car, the noise exploded.

Callum and Mateo found their way to me, and we all hugged each other tightly, taking comfort in one another.

"He's not going to get away with it," Callum vowed.

Mateo smiled grimly. "I paid Joey to put a tracker on his car. Payback for Everly's ring, and a way to track Saint."

"You're a genius!" I threw my arms around him, kissing him hard, and he laughed, before winding his arms around my waist and kissing me back.

"Don't forget we have an audience," he murmured.

Drawing back from him, I smiled. "I'm just glad that we can follow the car. Are you tracking it now?"

Holding up his phone to show me the screen with a map with a flashing dot on it, he nodded. "We'll get out of here as soon as we can. Don't thank me, though, thank Joey." He pointed toward a small dark-haired boy who looked to be around nine or ten years old, perched on top of a tire.

The boy waved, his lips curling up in a mischievous grin, before launching himself off the tire and running over to Esther. She swept him up into a hug, laughing.

"Esther's grandson," Callum said, in answer to my unspoken question.

I nodded, but my attention was taken by his phone screen with the map. "We need to get Saint back."

Callum stepped away from Mateo and I, conferring with a few of the people in the junkyard in a low tone. Eventually, he nodded and headed back over to us. "The junkyard will be taken care of. Let's get Saint back."

Finally.

Every second he'd been gone, I'd grown more and more worried for him. Even if the police commissioner didn't know what had happened to the mayor, it didn't mean he'd go easy on Saint. He'd arrested him; therefore, he had a plan. A plan that we needed to stop as soon as possible.

The three of us climbed inside the truck. Callum took the wheel, and Mateo sat next to him with the tracking app open on his phone. I was in the back, leaning forward between their seats, needing as good a view as possible.

Saint had been taken, and it was up to us to get him back.

We started off slow, following the route that the cop car had taken. The flashing dot on the map grew closer, but we still hadn't caught sight of the car.

"We need to stay back." Callum's voice was firm. "If he knows we're onto him, it could put Saint in danger."

"But what if he is in danger, and staying back makes it worse?" My mind filled with images of Saint, and the thought of him in pain made me physically hurt. He was strong, sure, but he had a soft heart. Callum and Mateo were harder, more callous than him. Of course, they all had their soft sides, and I'd been incredibly lucky to experience them, but there was something about Saint that was so caring and loving, and I hated the thought that someone could hurt him. Logically, I knew that he was capable of taking care of himself, and he wouldn't hesitate to harm anyone who he felt deserved it, but with the situation he was currently in, all I felt was concern.

"She's got a point." Mateo looked between us both. "Maybe we need a new plan."

Callum was quiet for a while, concentrating on following the moving dot, and then he cursed under his breath. "Okay. He's heading for the woods. Same place Lorenzo shot the mayor."

His jaw set, he gripped the steering wheel tighter. "You want a new plan? How does this sound?"

Then he floored the gas, shooting us forward so fast that the truck screamed and began to shake in protest.

"Hold the fuck on, brace yourselves, and make sure your seatbelts are fastened," he shouted, swerving us suddenly. I barely had time to take in the scene in front of me before we were coming at the police car side-on.

The impact threw me back against my seat, the screech of metal on metal reverberating all around us.

We came to a sudden stop, all of us breathing hard.

I raised my eyes to the scene in front of me.

The police car was stopped at an angle between two lanes of the road. Smoke—or at least, I assumed it was smoke—poured from the hood. The car alarm was blaring, but there was no one around to hear it, and the trees on either side muffled the sound.

The two figures inside the car began to move. Callum spoke again, his tone low and deadly, unclipping his seatbelt and placing his hand on the door.

"Let's end this. Now."

40

SAINT

You know, I wanted to say I was surprised by the way things went down, but we should have seen it coming. We had some calm moments, and now the storm was here.

"Saint Devin, you are under arrest for the murder of Robert Parker-Pennington II," the chief said as he headed toward me.

I was surprised that this murder was being put on me. As soon as the chief was next to me, he turned me around and pinned me to Esther's car.

"It's time for you boys to know your fucking place," he whispered. "I'm going to teach you not to stick your nose in somebody else's fucking business."

My heart began to accelerate as he put the cuffs on my wrists. He put them on so fucking tight I could already feel the metal biting my skin. He had no regard for my safety.

The people who were around us started to yell. I went quietly and without looking back, because having one of us blamed rather than all of us was best.

The chief was pissed since no one gave him the respect

he thought he deserved, and he pushed me inside of his car. He was showing me who had the power.

I fucking hated him.

"What, you're not going to read me my Miranda rights?" I questioned as he began to drive away.

Our eyes met through the rear-view mirror, and he smiled. "No need. You won't need them where you're going."

Fuck.

The asshole was way off the books now. It was my first clue when he didn't read me my rights. He wasn't thinking of taking me to the station for that reason alone. I could lawyer up, and he'd be fucked. I knew my brothers would have picked up on that too. It meant they had to move fast, because if I didn't make it to the station, this fucker would try and send me to hell.

"I can't go to hell yet; I have to graduate college first," I told him as I looked around, trying to see if I could find anything that could help me get out of this situation.

The chief glared at me.

I smiled at him.

"Since I know you have no plans to play this by the books. I am wondering how you are pinning the murder of the mayor, aka your boss, aka your partner, aka one-third of your human peddling ring, on me." I seethed the last part. "Or are you going to try and sell me off too?"

The chief's jaw was set in a hard line.

"Oh yeah, we know about that. I mean, that's why you wanted us quiet didn't you?"

"Your arrest is being spread like wildfire now. You'll lose that scholarship, be expelled from the college, and everything you worked hard for will disappear. You will be nothing."

My chest was rising and falling. I was trying to control

my anger. They wanted to ruin me, to soil my name so no one believed Cal and Mateo.

I needed to get answers from this dipshit while I was here. I had no doubt my brothers were coming, so I was going to treat this like an adrenaline ride.

Leaning forward as much as I could, I began to whisper in his ear, "Did you know the mayor was in bed with Lorenzo Rivas?"

The chief's body went stiff.

"How tragic must that be? For the mayor to betray his partners like that? Go ahead and kill me, but I would wonder what Lorenzo will do."

Now I was just talking out of my ass, but whatever rattled the fucker.

He didn't say anything this time, but I did see us pass the road that led to the precinct, so my guess had been correct.

"Out of curiosity, how did I kill your lover?"

He looked at me through the mirror, and it did nothing to diminish the hate in his stare. I continued, "All I knew was that he hadn't come home in a few days." I fake gasped. "No!" I shouted, making him jump. "He was cheating on you?"

"Shut up!"

"No," I barked back. "I'm bored."

I could see the veins on his neck begin to pop. I wondered if I could get him to have a heart attack. Would him losing control of the car kill me? Fuck it. It was worth a shot.

"Question," I went on as he took a sharp turn. Once I had composed myself, I kept going. "You only picked us up that day because you didn't want more people to ask questions about Erick's disappearance, right?"

The car had gone silent. I held my breath waiting for his answer.

"If the fucking mayor would have listened to me that night, I would have gotten rid of all of you."

I felt chills go down my body.

Then there was one thing that always kept nagging at me. "Why did you return his body?"

They disappeared people all the time. Erick could have been a missing person case that was never closed.

"I'm going to die anyway," I said, goading him. "Might as well give me the answers I crave."

He seemed to think on this and then began to speak, and I fought the urge to smile.

"The fucking dean and mayor thinking they were better than me just 'cause they had more money, when it was me doing everything."

"We all know Dean Walker doesn't get his hands dirty," I added, in hopes of feeding his hatred.

"I told them we should take care of that old bastard, but he started making a fuss about his stupid kid. Who knew deadbeat dads gave a shit."

My body felt like it was shaking, hearing him slander Dave's name. Sure, he had a problem, but he went to get help. I never saw the old man drink or smoke. He kept on being sober even after his kid was gone. The guilt he must have carried overshadowed his need for a relapse.

"You couldn't have some lowlife messing with a good thing?" I said slowly.

The chief looked back at me and gave me a cruel smile.

"No, we couldn't. A shame he wasn't like your mother. That would have made our lives easier."

My cool was wearing off. Unfortunately for me, now the fucker felt like being chatty.

"Records will show that the mayor lost his life trying to protect his child. When the three lowlifes that went to the college got him hooked on drugs, he did what any concerned father would have done and tried to confront them. You didn't like it, so you killed him." He looked at me again, and I could see the gleam in his eyes. "Everyone knows that the three of you stick together, so they will also lose everything."

This time it was my turn to smile.

"One little problem, though..." I scooted over as far as I could, even if it was hurting me. "We have a confession from the mayor."

His eyes went wide.

He had suspected we had something to do with him going missing. The three kids he had seen as nothing but pests had grown up.

But, of course, he had to have the last word.

"Do you know why your mother was with that boy the night we took him?"

I felt my blood drain. My ears rang. Everything was shaking. It took me a moment to realize that it wasn't just the shock that had me feeling this way, but the impact of something hitting us.

41

CALLUM

"Is everyone okay?" I rasped when I finally got my breath back, my ears ringing from the collision.

"Yeah. Fuck. Saint," Mateo groaned, pulling himself upright and reaching for the door handle.

"Saint," Everly echoed, and I turned to look at her. The airbags had been activated with the impact, but she seemed to be okay, other than her annoyed expression as she attempted to maneuver around the inflated bag.

Now I'd ascertained that the three of us hadn't sustained any injuries, I wasted no time in throwing open my door, running for the police car. Thick smoke was still billowing from the hood, and I shouted over my shoulder, "Stay back!" The last thing I wanted was for either of them to be caught up in an explosion.

The fucking windows were bulletproof glass—something that I knew from our contacts in the precinct. Before I could even think of what to do, Mateo was next to me, holding a crowbar.

Yeah. That would do it.

Together, we pried the back door open. Saint was frozen

for a minute, still in shock, and there was no time to waste. I gripped his arm and yanked as hard as I could.

He made a gasping sound, and then he was scrambling out, still cuffed, with his face bruised.

The three of us looked at one another, expressing how we felt without words.

We were alive.

The sound of the truck's engine starting up had us all spinning in place, like we were in sync. Everly was visible through the windshield as she backed the truck away from the danger zone, and we wasted no time in following her.

When we were all a safe distance away, watching the smoking police car, Everly turned off the truck engine and climbed out. She headed straight for Saint, throwing her arms around him. He couldn't hug her back, but I saw him press a kiss to the side of her head.

"Saint. Cuffs." Mateo was already prepared, brandishing the tool set we kept in the back of the truck. He worked on the cuffs, his brows drawn together, and eventually they clicked. He pulled them open with a look of triumph, freeing Saint's wrists.

Saint gave him a grateful smile, rubbing at his skin, before returning his attention to the now distant police car. The smoke was thickening, and I knew it was going to blow at any minute.

"It's a fitting end for this asshole," I commented.

Mateo nodded. "Two down—fuck!"

We all watched as the driver's-side door suddenly opened, and a dark shape streaked away, in the direction of the trees.

"Let's go!" I screamed, my legs already pumping, running in the direction the police chief had disappeared.

Everly, Mateo, and Saint were hot on my heels. The four

of us made it into the trees, and I came to a stop, breathing hard. When they stopped too, I placed a finger to my lips, listening intently.

There was a crack of branches up ahead, and I indicated my head in the direction the sound had come from. *Quiet*, I mouthed, knowing they'd follow me.

The second we started to move, there was a deafening explosion that ricocheted through the woods, and our surroundings were illuminated by a bright orange glow.

Everyone recoiled in shock, the sudden silence that followed the explosion seeming like it was deafening.

In the orange light, my eyes caught the figure streaking away, and I didn't even stop to think. I ran, harder than I'd ever run in my life.

"Cal! The ravine!"

Saint's voice had me skidding to a halt. Fuck. We were *here*. I hadn't realized how close we were.

The old man unfolded a map, spreading it across the table. "Here. This is a map of the local district."

The three of us crowded around as he used a pencil to outline areas. "Us. The south side. The north side. The university. The hospital." Gradually, his hand moved outward, until he was pointing out the road that led to Saint's mom's trailer park, and then he spun the map, his finger tapping on a large expanse of space.

"This here is the woods, and right in the middle, cutting them in half, there's a ravine." He traced over a long, jagged mark on the map. "Charles Blackstone was the founder of this town, but his surname came from here. The ravine is full of black stone. Dunno what stone it is, never cared to find out." A chuckle escaped him, before he turned serious again. "The point is, it's

dangerous. Slippery slopes, sharp, jagged rocks, and a river with ice-cold water. You boys stay away from that area, you hear me?"

I exchanged glances with Mateo and Saint, and we all nodded. The old man's face relaxed, and he blinked a few times. "Good." He cleared his throat. "You three are all I have left in the world, and I'm not going to lose you too."

"The ravine," I said aloud. "Okay. Spread out. Saint, come with me. Mateo and Everly, you take that side." I pointed to the left. "Let's round up this fucking bastard and teach him the history of Blackstone."

Everly and Mateo immediately moved in the direction I'd indicated, silent shadows, while Saint and I began moving forward. It was easy to hear the police chief up ahead—his labored breathing was loud in the silence that had fallen over the woods, not to mention the way he was crashing through the undergrowth, his movements growing more and more panicked as he realized he wasn't going to get away from us.

It was funny how things worked. One minute, this smug bastard was on top of the world—taking Everly, thinking he held all the cards, and the next...

We rounded a tree and there was the ravine in all its deceptively beautiful glory.

The next minute... would be the last for the police chief.

At least he'd have a good view when he died.

"Let me take care of this. I want to be the one to finish him off." Saint had caught up with us, and now the four of us made a solid line, blocking the police chief's path to safety. He had two choices—to step back and fall to his death, or to run at us.

The police chief's panicked gaze swung between us all.

"Not so confident now, are you?" I raised a brow.

"What did you mean when you said it was a shame the old man wasn't like my mom?" Saint spoke up at the same time.

The police chief ignored me, a humorless grin spreading over his face as he turned to Saint.

"You'll find out. Or maybe not. Frankly, I don't care either way." He took a step back, just as Saint took a step forward.

His lip curled, and his eyes burned. "See you in hell."

Then he jumped backward, off the edge of the ravine.

42

MATEO

Everything happened in slow fucking motion, from the moment we chased after the asshole chief, to the moment he looked back at us, smirked, and jumped.

Guess you had to respect him for that. He took his own life before we could do it. A part of me felt anger that he took that bit away from us, but then I turned to look at Everly and Saint, who seemed so fucking lost, and I was glad they had less blood on their hands.

Cal and I looked at each other. What did the chief tell him that had him so rattled? I'd find out later, but first we had to get out of here. Before they came looking for him, we needed to get away.

"We need to clear out," I said.

"Not yet," Cal added with a grimace. "We might need to clear our tracks."

Fuck, he was right.

The chief was crooked as shit, but he was still the chief of this town. And if we didn't get a handle on this, then the feds would get involved, and if they did, we were all fucked. Vigilante justice was still a crime.

Cal looked at Everly and then nodded toward Saint. Getting the hint, she took hold of his hand. He looked down at it and then pulled her to his chest.

"Wait in the car. The fewer tracks we leave behind, the better," I told them.

Neither of them argued, and they began to walk away.

"We need to call Lorenzo," Cal said. "He took two other squads to the garage."

"Yeah, I noticed, but they didn't follow him out here. They were more for intimidation," I added.

"I'm going to make sure there's no trace of us. Make the call. We have fifteen minutes at most before someone gets here. Reports from the blast probably made the ears of the cops."

He took off running again while I pulled the phone to my ear.

"*Compa*," Lorenzo greeted me on the third ring. "I'm starting to hear more from you than my own mother."

Although I found humor in what he said, I didn't have time for it right now.

"The same thing that happened at the yard happened right now," I spoke in code just in case. You never wanted to admit to murder over the phone.

Lorenzo whistled, knowing exactly what I was referring to.

"You boys are just swatting them like flies, aren't you?"

I stayed quiet.

"*Dejemen solo*," he told whomever of his men with him. "*Hablale a Rigo*."

Leave me alone and call Rigo, he told his men.

Once there was no more noise, he began to speak again.

"Who was it this time?" he asked.

When I still didn't speak, he sighed, annoyed.

"This line is secure. Hurry so I can see what I can do about it."

"The chief," I said as Cal was coming back.

He let out some curse in Spanish, but it took me a second to realize he was laughing.

"Call Rigo and give him your location. He will do the cleanup. I have a new chief I need to appoint. Thank you."

The line went dead.

Cal watched as I hung up, then called Rigo and immediately began to tell him where we were.

"He's taking over the cops in this town, isn't he?" Cal said.

I nodded. "Perfect opportunity. Let's get out of here. Rigo is going to do cleanup."

Whatever they said happened to the chief wouldn't include us. People in the south wouldn't care. Saint was free, and their community was still going strong.

When we made it back to the truck, Everly was raking her hands over Saint's hair. He had his hand on her shoulder. We all noticed the welts on his wrist. He had torn his skin.

"I'm okay," he spoke as we got in the truck. "Everly is letting me rest on her tits, so don't talk to me."

I could see the tension leave all of us.

As Cal drove us home, I knew I wasn't the only one thinking that the only one left standing was the dean. And I could bet my ass he had been the mastermind in this whole game. He preyed on the ambitions of those men, and used them while he kept his hands mostly clean.

When we pulled back to the yard, all the cars were gone. No tools were in sight and the garage was closed. Without words, we all got out and then opened the garage.

My throat constricted when I saw how everything was

put away. The buckets and rags we had used had been washed. Nothing was missing. Cal had asked them for a favor, and they'd all pulled through.

"We need to talk," Saint said as he led Everly to the couch. He sat down and then pulled her onto his lap. Cal turned the lights on as I closed the door again, and then we both stood in front of them.

"Tell us," Everly prodded.

"Remember how that homeless guy had said he had seen Erick arguing with a woman..." Saint went on, and we immediately knew what he was talking about.

"Yeah..." I spoke back, already having a sick feeling.

"It was Tiff, wasn't it?" Cal guessed, and based on the look on Saint's face, it was true. That's what he'd meant when he asked the chief that question.

Everly gasped.

Then I remembered what she had said when she came to visit.

"All you little assholes have always been a pain in my ass. Telling me what I can or cannot do with my baby."

She had meant friends, as in plural, and I knew Cal had never warned her, that was a first, and I only did it because she had pissed me off.

"Why would your mother be with Erick?" Everly questioned.

Tiff was a cunt, but she didn't gain anything from meeting him. And she was a lot of things, but she wasn't smart enough to be involved with something like this.

"I think that's my fault," Saint hissed.

"That bitch's actions aren't your fault," Cal told him, and we all nodded in agreement.

"Erick had asked me what the one thing I wanted the

most was... and back then the one thing I wanted the most was not to leave you guys. For Tiff to leave me alone."

I closed my eyes as it dawned on me. I knew it was clicking for Cal as well. It was so like fucking Erick to try and get Tiff to leave him. He would have probably tried to give her whatever little money he had.

"Do you hate me?" Everly took hold of Saint's face and forced him to look at her.

"Baby, you know I don't," he said honestly.

He then cast a look at us, and I knew what he wanted to say, but right now wasn't the time.

"My uncle is as close to me as you are to your mother. They are blood, yes, but they aren't family. We can't blame ourselves for their sins."

Fuck—this girl. She just knew what to say.

"Yeah, Tiff is a cunt. Don't drown in her mistakes," Cal said next.

"We'll always have your back," I reminded him.

He took a deep breath and then looked up at us with steel in his eyes.

"She's dead to me."

43

EVERLY

Two down, one to go. And then there was Tiff—where did she fit into the equation?

There were two things I was sure about. One: my uncle held all the rest of the answers. Two: we needed to act *fast*. There was a tiny window of opportunity remaining until all hell broke loose, and we needed to make sure that every single chess piece we had was in play.

So we slept for a few hours to regain some of our strength, and then, we planned.

For hours, the four of us worked, putting together all the pieces, building up a dossier of irrefutable evidence that would blow this operation wide open. Partway through, Lorenzo showed up with his right-hand man, who I found out was named Rigo, and they conferred quietly with Callum and Mateo, while Saint and I were compiling a list of potential accomplices, based on the information we had.

Lorenzo's eyes were sparkling with excitement as the discussion grew more animated, and I leaned closer to Saint. "Why do you think he's so excited?"

Saint followed the direction of my gaze, and smirked. "He wants power, and he knows that by taking down three of the most powerful men in Blackstone, their positions are open. It wouldn't surprise me if he ended up as the next mayor somehow, but whatever happens, I can guarantee that his men will be filling the free positions. He wants control, and he'll get it. Everything we're doing here is beneficial to him, one way or another."

"That makes sense." But then I remembered the look on his face when Callum had told him what we'd discovered. He'd been repulsed when he heard about the body parts of innocent victims, sold to rich people with no morals. "I think he cares a little bit, though."

Saint laughed. "He'd have to have a heart to care. I'm not sure he has one."

"That's what they said about the three of you," I reminded him. "But then I found out that you're all soft inside."

"Baby, there's nothing soft about me. In fact, why don't you harden me up even more?" Grabbing my hand, he pulled it between his legs and began rubbing it across his bulge. I screeched, snatching my hand away, both of us laughing even harder when we took in the raised brows of the others, who had stopped to stare at us.

"Nothing to see here. Carry on," Saint eventually said when we'd managed to calm down. I hadn't even known how much I'd needed to break some of the tension that had fallen over me, until then.

I leaned forward and placed a kiss to his cheek. "Thanks."

He shot me a wink. "Anytime."

Another hour passed, and I needed a break, so I decided

to go to the kitchen and see if I could find food for us all. I inspected the contents of the fridge—there were tons of energy drinks, which was good, but very little in the way of food. My paranoia wouldn't let me order anything—not that a delivery driver would be able to see inside the house, but even so. I grabbed an armful of the energy drinks, taking them back into the living room, and handed them out. Then, I asked to borrow Saint's phone. He gave it to me without hesitation, and I scrolled through his contacts, searching for the number I wanted, and copied it to my own phone. Then I headed back into the kitchen for privacy. I leaned back against the kitchen counter, waiting for the call to connect.

"Peaches Diner, Leah speaking."

"Hi. Could I speak to Esther please?"

"Who may I say is calling?"

"Everly Walker."

"One minute." She disappeared, and I could hear the noises of the diner's kitchen in the background—food sizzling, people calling out orders, the sound of pots and pans banging together.

Esther's voice came onto the line, full of concern. "Everly. Tell me our boy is safe."

"He's safe."

"Thank goodness." Her exhale of relief came loudly through the phone.

"He's safe," I repeated, "But we have a lot to do to ensure he stays safe. Not just him, all of us."

"What can I do?" She was suddenly all business.

"Well. There are six of us here at the junkyard right now, and the guys have been working really hard for hours without a break. I was wondering if we could get some food delivered. Do you do food delivery?"

"For my boys—and for you? Anything. I'll have some things brought right over. On the house."

"Thank you so much."

"Don't mention it. You just keep on taking care of my boys."

"I will," I promised, and I meant it.

Less than half an hour later, there was a knock at the door, and I opened it to find two guys, one holding four huge paper bags, and the other balancing a cardboard drinks holder with six drinks on it. I directed them into the kitchen where they dropped off the bags.

When they'd gone, I headed back into the living room. "Okay. Time for a break. That means *all* of you," I added when Callum frowned at me. "Come and get the food while it's hot."

"Food?" Saint immediately jumped to his feet. "I'm starving!"

Everyone trailed him into the kitchen, and soon the bags were open, and the guys were inhaling the food from Esther. The savory scent of burgers and fries, overlaid with the sweetness of milkshakes, filled the room.

"I fucking love Esther," Mateo mumbled around a mouthful of fries. He swallowed, then turned to me. "Thanks for doing this."

I shrugged, giving him a smile before popping a fry into my mouth. It was nothing, really; I was just glad to have a hand in lifting everyone's spirits after the traumatic events we'd all been through.

When the food was gone, everyone assembled back in the living room and got back to work. Almost an hour had passed when Callum spoke up.

"Okay, listen up. We have a plan."

As he spoke, my heart began to race. If we managed to

pull this off, we'd be ending my uncle's reign of terror and exposing his crimes to the nation in one fell swoop.

When he'd finished, he looked at each of us in turn.

"It's time to take down the last remaining piece on the chessboard, and win the game."

44
SAINT

Sleep did not come easy when you were waiting to go to war the next day. The only reason we could doze off for a bit was that our bodies were so exhausted, they were demanding it. The other thing on my mind preventing me from sleep was my mother. I mean, at this point I shouldn't have been surprised. She had been doing nothing but disappointing me all my life.

I rubbed a hand over my face and then reached for my phone. It was almost showtime.

When I heard a noise coming from the end of the hall, I got up.

Cal and Matty were there, and all the stuff in the old man's room was in boxes. It looked so barren now. He wasn't much for knickknacks, but taking down what little he had made a huge difference.

Both of them turned to look at me.

"We couldn't sleep," Mateo told me.

Yeah, I knew the feeling.

"Go get ready," Cal said.

Nodding, I headed to my room and grabbed a change of clothes. Everly walked in as I was about to put my shirt on.

"You're so beautiful," I felt the need to tell her.

She leaned against my doorframe and raised a brow at me. Her hair was still wet from her shower, and she was dressed simply in jeans and a shirt. Her face was void of makeup, but she had this glow about her that outshined everyone else.

"Come on." She held her hand out. "We need to go."

Ignoring her hand, I went for her waist and then hauled her over my shoulder. I was fine. I wasn't breaking. I guess I was just disappointed, which was a mistake on my part because Tiff had been doing that all her life.

"Put me down," Everly giggled.

I smacked her ass.

Mateo was right outside when I yelled at him.

"Catch."

His eyes widened for a second when I lightly threw Everly his way.

Her laughter was just what we needed. She leaned up and gave him a kiss, making him smile. Mateo kept lifting her up and down in his arms bridal style.

Callum was over by the truck, and he looked at all of us like we were idiots. Mateo ignored the look and then carried Everly over to him.

"Let's see if Cal has butterfingers," Mateo said before he passed her over to him.

Cal was quick to extend his hands. He caught Everly with ease as well, then gave her a kiss.

"We ride at dawn, bitches!" I yelled as I lifted one arm in the air.

No one was amused.

"Revenge and sex, guys," I told them as I walked into the truck.

"What about revenge and sex?" Mateo asked.

"Matty, it's like sex one-oh-one, everyone knows it's better if it's together."

"Are you planning to have sex with my uncle?" Everly teased.

Since she was up front, I settled for pinching her cheek.

"It's been so long since I last had pussy. My eyesight is weakening, my hearing is almost non-existent. I feel my hands begin to tremble. Baby, this is serious, you need to do something about it."

Everly giggled.

"Maybe you need a doctor," Cal snorted.

I fake gasped.

"Guys, the least you could have done was offer me a hand."

"You have two," Mateo scooted away from me.

Pouting, I looked at Everly.

"I'll offer you a hand." She smiled sweetly at me, and my dick got hard.

"Since we are on the topic," I began to say, and everyone was waiting to see what stupid shit came out of my mouth. That kinda hurt. "I have a complaint."

"A complaint?" Mateo raised his brows.

"Why am I being discriminated against?"

Their looks went from amusement to somewhat concerned.

"Why haven't I been allowed to fuck Everly's ass?"

Everly's cheeks flamed. Cal shook his head, and Matty sighed.

"Next time we are going to rock paper scissors for it."

"Stop the truck, Cal, I'll walk." Mateo pretended to try and get out of the truck.

Cal did not stop, in fact, he went faster.

"We all suffer together," he said.

I flipped them both off.

Next thing we knew, we were at school. And then the thing that we kept trying to not think about was finally going to happen. Cal parked close to the auditorium building. When planning our revenge, we never thought we could use the dean's position to our advantage, but here we were. The last remaining player in this fucking bloody game.

It was time to cut off his power.

He had lost his allies, so I bet he was rattled.

"Remember to stay together," Cal warned as we stepped off the truck. "He's about to have nothing to lose."

"We've got this," Everly said.

It was fucking go time.

"Bring it in, guys." I put my arm in the middle of all of them. "We want pussy, on thr—"

Mateo slammed my head to the side, but everyone was laughing. Which was good because we had been on edge all night.

We all walked into the auditorium where there was a ceremony going on. I just loved that the dean was there in all his glory, smiling and thinking he was better than everyone else. Once inside, we stuck to the back, keeping to the shadows.

"How long now?" I asked Cal.

He was sending a message.

"Just waiting on confirmation from my guy."

We kept on moving, knowing we didn't have much time.

We knocked on the door to the media room and a guy stepped out.

"We are going to get justice for your friend," Mateo told him.

The guy nodded and then stepped out.

Inside the room, Cal and Everly rushed to get the projector to mirror what was going to play on Cal's phone. Mateo stood guard at the door while I watched the stage.

"Perfect," I said as the dean took the podium.

Cal's guy came through, and we knew this because not only did Cal's phone go off, but also the phones belonging to everyone who was connected to the university's databases.

People looked around. The dean, being the professional that he was, had no idea what was going on, but he kept trying to get them to calm down.

I pulled out my own phone and saw where the recording was coming from.

Countless names and files. Missing people reports, then comparing them to the reports on the school.

That was when Cal put the projector on.

"And the person responsible for these heinous crimes," the monotone computer voice the hacker had injected into the display said, "is none other than your precious dean."

Hell broke loose as the people in the auditorium gasped, and looked up at the stage, terrified.

"Checkmate," Everly said.

45

CALLUM

In all the commotion, it took me a minute to realize that the dean was no longer up on the stage. The second I noticed he'd gone, I was running toward the stage, closely followed by Everly, Mateo, and Saint. I completely ignored the uproar as I headed straight into the wings and then into the backstage area.

It was chaos back here too—people running around, shouting into phones, furiously texting. I had no doubt the news was spreading like wildfire. This story was *huge*.

We'd taken care to keep our names out of it, although we knew reporters would eventually come sniffing around, with Erick's name on the list. But the old man was gone, with his death officially listed as a heart attack, so I had a feeling the reporters would be most interested in Everly. She was the only living relative of the dean, after all. We'd talked long and hard about what the repercussions might be of making this information public, but Everly had been insistent that we share it with the world.

We'd do everything in our power to protect and shield her, although it was becoming very clear that she was more than capable of standing up for herself. Our queen wore her crown well.

"He went that way." One of the guys backstage indicated toward the door that led to the back exit of the auditorium. Giving him a nod of thanks, I increased my pace, racing down the corridor and bursting out of the door in time to see the dean's car pulling away from the staff parking lot with a screech.

"Fuck!" My shout reverberated off the buildings.

"Callum. Tracker, remember?" Everly slid her arm around me, and I was instantly calmer. *Of course.* That had been part of our plan. It had been more or less guaranteed that her uncle would try to get away, and we'd taken steps to ensure we could still find him. One of Lorenzo's men was watching his house, and they'd also paid off the guard so they could sneak into the gated community and plant a tracker on his car. Wherever he went, we wouldn't be far behind.

"Yeah." I glanced down at her, placing a quick kiss to her forehead. "Thanks, baby. We have no time to lose. Let's get to the truck."

The four of us ran for the student parking lot, but when we neared it, I made us slow down. The wasted seconds were torturous, but this way, if any of the parking lot cameras caught us, they wouldn't suspect anything out of the ordinary. Saint got way too into the act in my opinion, hauling Everly onto his back and running around the cars, laughing, while Mateo and I went through the rest of the plan once again, knowing that the cameras didn't pick up sound, only movement.

Mateo's phone sounded, and he quickly glanced at the screen. "Lorenzo's tracking the car too. Just received confirmation."

"Good. Everything's going to plan so far." I was sure it wouldn't be this simple for long, because when was anything easy when it came to these three fucking bastards? We'd prepared as much as we could, though, and now all we could do was follow through with the rest of our plan and hope that it went in our favor.

The second we were in the truck with the doors closed behind us, I pulled up the tracking information, settling my phone in the cradle I had mounted on the dash. He was ahead of us, but he couldn't run forever. Sooner or later, we'd catch up to him. The truck's tank was full of gas, the trunk had all the supplies that we could think of that might come in useful, and we were ready to follow him wherever he went. With Lorenzo as our backup, our odds were as good as they could get.

Lowering my foot to the accelerator, I gave a grim smile.

"Let's do this."

"He's heading out of town for sure." Mateo was alternating between focusing on the tracker with a laser stare and texting updates to Rigo. We'd triangulated our positions, coming at the dean from either side, but if he got on the highway, it would be a straight-up chase. I suddenly wished for dickhead Robbie's Lambo—the dean's car would have no chance against it.

But our truck was fast, despite its weight, thanks to the engine tuning we'd done. We were gaining on him.

We hit the outskirts of Blackstone, and then it was just the highway up ahead.

"Tell Lorenzo to stay back. It looks like he's slowing

down a little, and if he's up to something, we don't want him to see we're following him. He'll recognize our truck."

Mateo relayed the information to Rigo, then put his phone on speaker. Lorenzo's voice sounded through the truck's interior.

"I'll come up ahead of you. He won't recognize my car, and you'll be behind me, so he won't notice anything out of the ordinary."

"Got it." I nodded at Mateo to end the call, then I eased up on the gas, letting Lorenzo's car get ahead of us. He was driving some piece-of-shit-looking nondescript station wagon, but I'd personally worked on that car, and I knew what lay under the hood meant that its outer appearance was deceptive.

When Lorenzo was in place, I kept a safe distance, my gaze focused on the road. It was easy to see now that we were steadily gaining on the dean, and my tight grip on the steering wheel eased incrementally.

We passed the trailer park, and my gaze flicked to Saint's in the rear-view mirror. His mouth was set in a flat line, a serious expression on his face that I rarely saw. Fuck, I wished I could take away the pain that I knew he'd always felt when it came to his mom. She was a fucking leech, always taking and never giving anything in return, and yet his big heart meant that he kept giving to her, time and time again. His joking hid a lot of the hurt, but I knew him too well. He was my brother, and I'd do anything for him. The only reason I hadn't taken out Tiff myself was because he still clung on to her. Or not to her, but to the idea of her. To the knowledge that he had a parent who was alive, while the rest of us didn't, and I think his guilt about that was one of the reasons he had trouble letting go.

But with the revelations we'd had over the past few days,

I knew that something had changed. Something deep inside him. In his head, he'd cut those ties for the final time, and I was so fucking proud of him.

Shaking myself out of my thoughts, I realized that we were slowing down even more, and I quickly pumped the brakes before I ran into the back of Lorenzo's car.

"The truck stop." Everly was leaning forward between the seats, pointing ahead. "Do you think that's where he's going?"

We watched as the dean's car, now clearly visible, took a turn. It wasn't quite the truck stop—it was what looked like a service road, dusty and disused, running up the side of the truck stop. I followed Lorenzo into the truck stop itself, where we came to a halt down the side of the building, out of view of any cameras. Our truck filled with silence as we watched the moving dot slow, then stop, not too far away.

I took a deep breath. "Okay. Looks like we've reached our final destination. Let's end this."

46

SAINT

It was finally happening. That moment we'd dreamed of since we were kids was finally about to be achieved.

The thrill of the chase was a high I didn't think I'd ever forget. I was so wrapped up in that feeling, that when we passed by the trailer park, I felt nothing.

There were no more mixed feelings.

I had felt guilty for discarding a mother when I still had one, but the thing was, Tiff never thought of me as her son. She took and took, and now there was nothing left for me to give her other than my hatred. At least I wouldn't have any regrets in my life. I closed my eyes, and I couldn't recall one fucking time where she ever did anything for me.

"—let's end this."

I snapped out of my thoughts as soon as Cal spoke, and I looked ahead. The final piece in this sick fucking game was about to be dethroned. *It took years, Erick, but we finally did it.* I'd like to think he and the old man were looking down at us and giving us all their support.

The place looked to be deserted, with no cameras and

no people; only us, Lorenzo, and Rigo. Justice was about to be served.

We all got out of the truck, trying not to run in guns blazing.

"Be careful," Mateo reminded us.

We went in groups of two—Mateo and I ahead of Cal and Everly, with Lorenzo and Rigo at our backs.

Blackstone was a fucking mess right now, that no one would care about this bloodshed. Its leader had disappeared, and people would think he'd done it before the ship he and the dean were on had begun sinking—the same for the chief. All the loose ends were tying up nicely.

Where the fuck did the dean go? What business did he have here?

We all rounded a corner, when I stopped dead in my fucking tracks. Yeah, the dean was there, but so was fucking Tiff. I knew I wasn't the only one at a loss, because everyone stopped where they were. The place had a fence surrounding it, and if they wanted to leave, it would be from the same place they came in.

"*Que paso?*"

From the little Spanish I knew, Lorenzo had just asked what was going on.

"That's my mother," I said in a monotone voice. Nothing that bitch did could shock me anymore.

"I don't get it," Everly hissed.

"You like your mother?" Rigo asked as he pulled out his gun. He and Lorenzo looked the happiest out of all of us.

I could feel everyone's eyes on me. And I knew my brothers and Everly wouldn't judge me for the decision I made. They had my back no matter what. I took a deep breath, knowing time was running out.

"She's no family of mine," I told them.

"Let the fun begin." Lorenzo smiled as he pulled out his piece. He then handed Mateo and Callum a gun each. Something that wouldn't be traced back.

"Let's do this," Cal murmured.

It looked like Tiff had brought shit for the dean. She was handing him stuff. From their body language, this wasn't their first meeting. The asshole was an outcast by now, and I guess to survive, he needed a fucking leech to show him the way—Tiff was ideal.

Just then, two gunshots were fired at the same time. The sounds ricocheted in the emptiness, causing my ears to pop, but I kept running, as did Cal, Mateo, and Everly. The tires on the car blew up, so it would make it impossible for the dean to go anywhere.

At the same time, they stared at where we were coming from with wide eyes. My mother looked at the dean and then at me.

The dean also looked at us, and then he looked at Everly with disgust. He acted quickly, grabbing Tiff by the throat, and putting her in front of him.

"You kill me, you have to kill her," he shouted.

Cal slowly waved his hand so I wouldn't speak right away. They wanted to play with their prey, and after years of staving for this, I couldn't have agreed more.

"How does it feel to be the most hated—" Cal started saying.

"Most wanted," Mateo taunted.

"Man in town," I finished.

The dean was glaring at us, and his eyes had a manic look to them. Everything he had worked for had tumbled down right before his eyes, and all thanks to the girl who brought us the missing pieces. The queen of this game—his niece.

"Everly," he barked. "Your father woul—"

Our girl roared.

"Don't you dare bring my father's memory into this!" She took a deep breath. "You always felt so high and mighty, and you were the worst kind of monster. My father would have wanted you stopped."

"Baby," I heard Tiff wheeze out.

"Why are you helping him?" I asked, not sure I cared at this point.

"He has lots of money, baby. I was just doing this for the money."

A sinister laugh escaped my lips.

I felt the warmth of a small hand wrap around me. The fucking dean's eyes were livid now, looking at where Everly was holding on to Cal and me.

"You should have been grateful that I gave you a place to stay—"

"With money you made from trafficking people," Everly seethed. "Blood money."

I looked at my mother, who seemed to think I was going to save her.

"I don't even want to know why you were with Erick that night, I already figured it out. And that's how you know the dean, isn't it? They paid you off to keep quiet."

Her bulging eyes were enough.

"May you rest in peace, Mother."

At that moment, the dean's and my mother's eyes went wide with fear, knowing that we were not going to negotiate. I held Everly's hand tighter as the rest of them pulled out their guns and shot.

47

EVERLY

It all happened so quickly. One minute, Tiff was there, being used as a human shield, the next, she was crumpled to the ground, a bullet between her eyes. Lorenzo didn't waste a breath, shooting out my uncle's kneecap the second she was out of the way. He didn't even stand a chance.

His scream was something that would haunt my dreams, but he deserved every single bit of pain. Too many innocents had suffered and bled under his hands.

As if they'd rehearsed it, the guys all looked to me, and I gave a single nod. They were giving me a chance to get closure before they finished it off.

Taking a deep breath, I straightened my shoulders and clenched my fists at my sides, and then made my way over to my uncle with slow, purposeful movements. He'd fallen, clutching his knee, tears of pain streaming down his face. When he raised his eyes to mine, something like disappointment clouded his gaze.

"We... could... have... worked so well... together," he

ground out between clenched teeth. "You could... have been... rich."

I laughed without humor. "You think I'd ever want a part in your sick operation? I would rather die than be involved in anything to do with this." Stepping right up to him, I narrowed my eyes. "How did Tiff get here? Why were you meeting her?"

He clamped his mouth shut, but his eyes darted to the left, and I stretched out my arm in the direction of his gaze. Keeping my gaze fixed on my uncle, I spoke, loud enough for my voice to carry.

"Anyone want to check if there's something hiding over there? Another vehicle, maybe?"

Something flickered in my uncle's gaze, and I smiled. *Bingo.*

I heard footsteps behind me, and then Lorenzo came up on my left, Callum to my right. Callum placed his hand on my lower back, a warm, reassuring presence, while Lorenzo kept his gun trained on my uncle.

"Look at you," my uncle bit out. "You've got them acting like trained dogs. One day, you'll learn that even the best trained dog can turn on its owner."

Slowly, I shook my head. "There are so many things wrong with that statement. I don't even know why I'm wasting my breath explaining, but I will. One: they're not trained dogs. We are a team. We work together. And that brings me to point number two. They wouldn't turn on me, because we have trust. We—"

He spat in the direction of Lorenzo. "You trust *him*? He'd slit your throat in your sleep."

From next to me, Lorenzo cleared his throat. "Everly has earned my respect. My people like her. She's proven her loyalty to the south side. End of discussion." In a lightning-fast move, he stepped forward and pistol-whipped my uncle across the mouth.

My uncle screamed, spitting blood and what looked like a tooth onto the dirt at our feet. Lorenzo's lip curled, but he remained otherwise impassive.

"Why did you do it?"

There was barely any point in me asking the question. Either way, my uncle was going to die here today. But I needed to know.

"Money. Power," he garbled out, blood bubbling from his lips. He still managed a smile, glaring at me with defiance, and in that moment, I was actually thankful that my parents were no longer around. My dad would never have to deal with the fact that his own brother had become a monster.

I took a step back from him, Callum's hand still on my lower back, keeping me steady.

"You wanted money and power, but instead, you brought about death and destruction. Your name will be tainted forever in this town. In this state. In the entire USA, in fact. Is that the kind of legacy you wanted to leave?" I didn't wait for him to reply, but continued, "I renounce you as my uncle. You're dead to me."

"Everly." His voice turned pleading, and I closed my eyes, sucking in a shuddering breath.

"Look at me, baby." Callum removed his hand from my back, and grasped my face between both hands, turning me away from him. I looked into his blue eyes, and they were calm and steady. "I'm so fucking proud of you. We *all* are."

He seemed to realize that I was close to losing it, the toll of the day threatening to take me under. "Keep your eyes on me." His thumb stroked across my cheek. "Hold on for just a little longer."

"Now?" Lorenzo spoke up. Everyone ignored my uncle's babbling pleas.

Callum nodded once, never looking away from me.

A gunshot rang out, and there was an abrupt silence, followed by a dull thump that I knew was the sound of my uncle's body hitting the dirt.

Callum gathered me into his arms. "It's over now," he said, and I finally let myself fall apart.

By the time I'd pulled myself back together, Lorenzo and the body were gone. Callum drew back, looking down at me. "Are you feeling up to coming to see something?"

I nodded, giving him a tremulous smile. He lowered his head to give me a soft kiss, then released me, but threaded his fingers through mine. "Come with me then."

Lorenzo reappeared from around the truck stop, and he gave Callum a nod, then fell into place next to him. We walked in silence, down the old service road, until we rounded a corner, and came across a battered white van. The back doors were open, and sitting or standing around it were four children, ranging in age from around seven or eight up to fifteen. Each of them had the same scared, slightly disbelieving expressions on their faces, with huge, untrusting eyes, and it broke my heart.

Mateo was crouched next to one of the smaller boys, and after tousling his hair, he rose, coming over to us. "These kids would have been lost forever if it wasn't for you. You saved them."

The lump in my throat was so big that it took me a few tries to speak. "*I* didn't save them. *We* saved them. All of us did."

Saint had been wrapping a blanket around a teenage girl's shoulders, and now he came to us, taking my free hand. "You did so good. We're so proud of you."

"I'm proud of you. All of you," I said fiercely. "You guys mean everything to me."

Lorenzo and Rigo were conferring in low voices over to my left, and as soon as I stopped speaking, Lorenzo headed over. "It would be best for you to get out of here now. The cleanup crew is on the way, and we have someone lined up to take care of the kids until we can get everything straightened out."

"Who?" Saint eyed him with suspicion.

He grinned and it made him look surprisingly carefree and boyish. "Esther."

My heart warmed. Esther would take good care of them. It seemed all my guys approved, because smiles spread across all three of their faces, and it was like the sun coming out. Suddenly, I felt like I could breathe again.

I met each of their gazes in turn—brown, then green, then blue—and I could see the relief in each of their eyes. "This is really over, isn't it?"

Callum nodded. "It's over. Let's go home."

48

MATEO

It was finally over.

The sick feeling I'd been carrying inside me since Erick and Dave left had disappeared. I suddenly felt lighter, like I could finally breathe.

Add the fact that we'd rescued kids from being trafficked after we killed the fucker; it made it all that much sweeter.

The whole town was in a frenzy, reeling from the fact that their beloved leaders had done despicable things. We didn't want the feds to come looking, but we had wanted justice to be served, so we bent the rules in our favor.

We burned all the information on the people who bought from the dean. That was one problem we didn't need to come to bite us in the ass. No one but the rich could afford organs from the black market. It was a Pandora's box. We kept the names of the lost ones and all the other information had been released. Just enough evidence to sink the dean's reputation, a tally of his victims, because they had already been forgotten, but they needed their memories to be kept alive since the mayor, the dean and the chief stole their lives from them.

Living after revenge was served was sweet.

"So, what's going to happen with the positions?" Saint asked.

We were all hard at work. It was like our bodies hadn't caught up with the fact that we were finally safe. We just kept moving.

"They're going to be temporarily filled," Callum said. "Well, the school will appoint a new dean, but the people will vote for the next mayor in the upcoming election next year."

"That's why Lorenzo has been at the forefront trying to get justice," Everly added.

"Open the window," I yelled to Saint so he could do it before this room became a mess.

Cal and I began to rip the old carpet from the old man's room—well, our room now. We came home, slept, and then began to work on the room. Now that we had a fresh start, we decided we were ready to finally let go of all our ghosts. The bedding had gotten here a few days ago, but with everything going on, we had ignored it.

"Mamas," I called out to get Everly's attention. "Did you make up your mind about where we're setting up the bed?"

She blushed.

"It doesn't matter."

Saint was closest to her, and he grabbed her by the waist and kissed the side of her head.

"We told you that you are the queen of this castle."

She took a minute and then pointed to where she wanted it to go.

We kept on working for a little longer before we got ready. There would be a memorial later that the city had put together. Since everything was in chaos, we'd finally taken some days off to finally catch our breaths.

Everly's and Saint's phones kept going off like crazy since they were the ones with friends. Saint's phone went off again. Being the impatient person that he was, he would read the messages but not text back, except this one had him doing a double take.

"Holy shit," he breathed.

All our heads turned to him.

"What happened?" Cal was the first one to say, both of us already on alert.

"Now that the mayor is no longer here, they impeached Robbie from being frat president. That's not all—the school is flooded with complaints against him and all the shit he did because he thought he was untouchable."

The three of us looked at one another. We had planned to take care of him, but I guess that was one name off our shit list. And honestly, we didn't care about him enough to bother with him now. At the end of the day, the only ones with Everly were us.

"Mamas, go shower." I nodded toward the bathroom.

She squinted her eyes because she knew we were up to something.

"Anyone wants to join me?" She strutted out of the room, then turned her head, giving us a come get me look.

"We start with you, baby. We won't be leaving the house for a week," I said when I saw Saint's resolve begin to fade.

She looked at all of us but then walked away.

"I hate you guys," Saint hissed.

"Tonight," Cal reminded him.

As soon as we heard the water run, we got the shit together that we'd hidden in the garage, and then ran to the heart of the maze and began to set it all up.

"Now that Robbie is being dealt with, what will we do about that bitch?"

"Let's tell Everly," Cal told us as I passed him an extension cord. "Our girl can handle anything."

The pride in his tone was the same way we all felt.

"Pusssaaaaaay tooooonight," Saint began to sing as he humped the air left and right.

He then stopped and pointed to the both of us.

"Let's do it now before we ruin the moment later."

Cal gave me a confused look, but I knew what he was talking about.

"Best two out of three wins," he told us as he extended his arm, ready for rock paper scissors.

A few hours later, we were standing in front of our old foster house. On the way here we had a talk with Everly, something we didn't want to do but she needed to know the information. She didn't say anything except that she would handle it.

The building still looked the same, and even if I rode around Blackstone, this was one place I'd never been back to. The four of us were standing together. The crowd was huge. Everyone from the south was there, with many people from the other side, proof that people were capable of coming together amidst tragedies.

Everly was standing in front of me, with my hands on her waist. She held on to Cal and Saint with her hands, knowing that we needed support.

Flowers and candles were spread everywhere, along with pictures upon pictures of boys and girls that had been missing from this town. There was a podium, and we waited for the speech to commence. We were happy to take a back seat. We had wanted justice, but we weren't fans of glory. That wasn't our style. All we wanted was a peaceful life.

It was getting darker by the time we heard a commotion at the front.

"How is that the same guy?" Everly hissed, amused.

Lorenzo walked up, looking unlike anything we had ever seen before. He wore a fitted gray suit. His dark hair had been styled, and the stern look on his face was nowhere in sight. This was just another stepping stone on his agenda.

"Matty, if he can clean up nicely, so can you," Saint whispered.

"Fuck off," I replied.

We stayed quiet as Lorenzo began to speak.

"For so long, we have been divided. Our leaders drove that wedge deeper and deeper because we wouldn't have time to be at war with them if we were at war with each other. I'm sick and tired of seeing the kids of our community disappear. Kids who aren't guilty of any crimes, but all because they grew up alone... poor... with parents who made mistakes they got blamed for. I'm tired of seeing the future of our community struggle."

The people roared.

"We are here today to honor the lives of all those who disappeared. Of all of those who were killed!" he spat with a passion that surprised even me.

"We are here to remember them. Say their names with me, and let's never let them be forgotten again. Let's do better for ourselves... for our future."

Everyone chanted, and then the bastard let them settle before speaking again.

"As a campaign gift from me to you, to all of us, we will rename the park across the street as the Erick Evans Memorial Garden."

My throat constricted, and I had to blink back tears.

"Because it only takes one match to set a fire," he finished saying.

The south would know what we did. They loved Dave, and they respected us. They would know there wasn't anything you wouldn't do for family.

I kissed the top of Everly's head.

"Let's go home," Cal said.

49

EVERLY

We stepped back and began making our way around the clusters of people facing the podium. It was time to leave. We'd paid our respects, and now I needed to just be with Callum, Mateo, and Saint—just the four of us, together and ready to begin our future.

When we reached the back of the crowd, I spotted a couple of familiar faces and stopped abruptly. I was holding Mateo's hand, and he shot me a look as I came to a sudden halt. "What is it?"

I released my grip on him. "You guys go ahead. This won't take a minute."

When I neared Hallie and Mia, Mia gave me a broad smile, but Hallie must have seen something in my eyes, because her face paled, and she took a step back.

"Hi, Mia." I spared my friend a genuine smile, before turning to Hallie. My voice turned as cold as ice. "Hallie."

Hallie swallowed hard, and Mia's eyes widened, her gaze flicking from me to Hallie. "What's going on, Everly? We came to pay our respects."

"I appreciate that. More than you know." Laying a hand

on her arm, I squeezed lightly, before returning my attention to my former friend. "Hallie? Why are you here?"

She stammered for a minute, and when she realized that I wasn't going to magically warm up to her, it was like all her bravado was suddenly stripped away. "Everly, I—"

"No." I held up my hand. "There's no excuse for you helping to spread rumors about me and siding with Robbie, right at the time I needed my friends the most."

Mia gasped from next to her, staring between us. "Hallie? What?"

Hallie seemed to snap. "So what? She took them from me, Mia! Don't you care? She took them all for herself!"

Both Mia and I recoiled at the venom in her tone. Mia recovered quicker than I thought she would, her eyes turning hard as she placed her hands on her hips. "Excuse me? First of all, Everly didn't take anyone. You were never with any of the Boneyard Kings. They'd never even given you the time of day before Everly came along, had they? And no, I don't care, because Everly's happy with them, and that's what matters to me. Seriously, Hal? Are you that fucking jealous that you had to try and sabotage Everly's happiness?"

Hallie gaped at her, and I bit back a surprised smile. I'd hoped Mia would remain on my side, but I hadn't expected her to turn on Hallie so easily.

"Robbie's gone, and I think it's time for you to leave." I lowered my voice. "I wish that things had gone differently, but hey, we all make our own choices, and you chose to stab me in the back. I'm not interested in vengeance—I just want a quiet life. But I'm warning you right now, if you stick around? My three boyfriends will more than likely make your life hell. They're very... protective of me."

Tears filled Hallie's eyes, even as she glared at me. "Fine!

I hate it here, anyway. You won't see me again." Then she spun away from Mia and I, pushing her way out of the crowd.

Mia caught the expression on my face, and instantly moved to hug me. "Hey. Don't feel bad. Hallie's an adult. No one is responsible for her actions except her. She has to be prepared to pay the price."

I hugged her back hard. "Thank you. You're the best."

She laughed against me. "Don't you forget it." Drawing back, she met my eyes. "Call or text me tomorrow, okay? And if you ever need anything, you know I'm always here, right?"

I nodded. "I know. Same. Always."

We hugged again, and then I released her. "I'd better go."

"Go."

When I'd taken a few steps, she called after me. "If the Boneyard Kings have any hot friends I haven't met yet, introduce me, okay?"

A smile spread across my face as I lifted my hand in a wave. "Okay. Take care of yourself, Mia. I'll speak to you tomorrow."

The truck pulled up outside our home. Saint helped me out, not that I needed it, but it seemed like all three of them wanted to be close to me today. I felt the same. Maybe it was the memorial, remembering those who were lost, and reminding ourselves of what we still had. Or maybe it was the fact that our relationship had become so close, so deep, that I knew that nothing could ever come between us.

"Wanna shower and change, then come outside?" Saint pushed me gently toward the house, and with a smile, I followed his instructions. A short, flowy red dress was laid out on our new bed when I came out of the bathroom, and I pulled it on, pairing it with my Vans because if they expected me to go out into the dirt-filled junkyard, I was going to protect my feet.

The three Boneyard Kings were standing outside the house waiting for me, dressed in variations of their work clothes—overalls and baggy pants, with heavy boots. I took a moment to drink in the sight of them, all of them looking so sexy in the fading sunlight, before I made my way over to them.

Callum stepped behind me. "Do you trust us?" he murmured into my ear, and when I nodded, he placed a length of cool, silky material around my eyes, tying it at the back of my head. They led me along, into the maze of wrecked cars, if my sense of direction was anything to go by, moving deeper and deeper into the stacks, until we eventually came to a stop.

I felt hot breath on the side of my face, and then Saint's voice was whispering in my ear, "Are you ready for this?"

"Yes. I'm ready."

I heard Mateo's low chuckle, and then his hands were on my face, gently caressing my skin, before he moved his hands around to the back of my head to undo my blindfold.

The sun was setting, dipping down behind the piles of cars. As the scene in front of me came into view, I gasped out loud, my hand flying to my mouth.

"This... this is..." I swallowed hard, looking between them all. "I love you. All of you. So, so much."

50

SAINT

This was how we should have done this the first time. Funny how life came full circle and let us right our wrongs. We were back in the same place we once tried to humiliate Everly, but it was to do the opposite this time. We wanted to show her she was our world. Maybe she knew already, but we needed to get the words out. It was like they tried to claw their way out, but it hadn't been the right moment.

We fucking loved this girl.

The center of the maze was surrounded by fairy lights, a thick blanket in the middle, and a basket with some food for later. Mateo took off the blindfold, and those doe eyes we loved so much went wide, and they shined with something that made me start to lose control.

"I love you. All of you. So, so much."

Fuck.

My emotions went flying all over the place. I had heard those words before. I knew what they meant, but I had never had someone direct them at me.

Those words finished filling a space inside me that I

wasn't aware I had. Judging by my brothers' faces, I knew they felt the same way.

"Say it again," Cal rasped out.

Out of all of us, he was the only one who didn't remember his parents. Those words meant the world to him.

Everly took a step forward and then reached onto her tiptoes.

"I love you, Cal."

The words were barely out when he started to swallow her confession. His arms went around her waist and a hand curved down to her ass, gripping her through her sexy red dress.

I groaned because my dick was like, *me first*.

"How about me, mamas? You love me too?" Mateo circled around and began to kiss her neck.

Cal used the opportunity to move his hands down to her thighs. He pushed her dress higher and higher, revealing her creamy white skin.

Everly opened her mouth to speak, but Mateo tipped her head back and stuck two of his fingers into her mouth, making her gag.

"Next time you tell us, we want you to scream it," Mateo said.

I could hear her moaning around Mateo's fingers as Callum fingered her pussy.

Mateo whispered something in her ear, and she nodded her head. Mateo lifted her, and then Cal removed her panties. The dress went next, and our girl was naked before us.

Knowing all eyes were on her, she walked to the center of the blanket and began to kneel.

"Why are you guys wearing clothes?" she questioned as her hand disappeared between her legs.

Fuck.

The three of us began to get naked. My dick sprang free, ready to fuck her into oblivion. We moved around her, surrounding her like we did the last time we were here. The only difference was that this time, she had all the power.

Her moans got louder when she saw that we were jerking off.

I stepped closer, not being able to stand it anymore. I gripped her wrist to stop her from fingering herself, then pulled out her hand. She was fucking wet and smelled delicious. I pulled her fingers into my mouth, licking off her juices.

"So fucking hot," Cal murmured.

Everly pulled back and laid down with her legs wide open.

This time it was me who smiled wickedly.

"Oh no, baby, on all fours."

She bit her lip and started to do that, but Cal stopped her. He laid down next to her, and then, in one fluid movement, he moved her on top of him. With one loud thrust, he entered her. Everly's head fell back in pleasure as she let out a moan.

"Your pussy feels like fucking heaven," Cal told her as he began to fuck her harder. Everly held on to his shoulders as she matched his thrusts and rode him. Shit, I was going to come from just looking at them.

Mateo kneeled next to them and reached for Everly's head, guiding her mouth to his dick. They both filled her as she gasped around them—all of them finding pleasure in each other.

I stepped closer to them, watching them love each other, and I couldn't take it any longer. Bringing two fingers into my mouth, I sucked them until they were nice and wet. With my other hand, I pushed against Everly's back a bit. Noticing what I wanted, she positioned herself so I could have her ass.

Fuck yeah.

Cal moved his legs so I could have some room.

"Do you like this, baby?" I asked her as I teased her hole. "Being loved by all of us."

She moaned her answer against Mateo's dick.

He chuckled, because none of us could understand what she was saying. The only thing we knew was that she loved the fact that we were owning her.

I inserted one finger inside her. She was so fucking warm and tight, I couldn't wait to fuck her there.

Mateo pulled her hair, and she released his dick with an audible pop.

"We asked you a question, mamas," he said in a husky tone.

I pulled my finger back, only to thrust it back in faster.

Everly let out a strangled moan.

"I love it."

My finger began to move faster. I added another. Then I grabbed my dick and teased her hole, letting my precum finish lubricating her.

"Who do you belong to?" Cal asked her as I began to slowly push my way inside of her.

Everly held her breath as I filled her up.

"Don't make us ask again," Mateo growled.

"You," she hissed when I finished sliding all the way in.

"Who?" I managed to say as I began to move in sync with Cal.

"The Boneyard Kings—" She barely got the words out when we all fucking lost it.

Mateo began to fuck her mouth. I could see tears springing to her eyes, and I could feel her contractions as she got closer to her release.

"She fucking loves this," Cal groaned as he began to fuck her harder.

"That mouth, baby, I'm not going to last," Mateo told her.

Both Cal and I held on to her hips as we continued to fuck her. Mateo had her hair wrapped around his arm, so he could watch as we fucked her while she sucked him off.

"Fuck," I hissed as I began to come.

I knew they weren't far behind, because I could feel Everly coming, and I knew Cal wouldn't last either.

We all just stayed there for a moment, catching our breaths.

Matty pulled back and then kneeled to be at eye level with Everly.

"In case it wasn't obvious, we love you too," he told her.

I kissed her spine and then pulled back.

Cal laid her down next to him.

"I love you," he whispered as he pushed back tendrils of hair from her sweaty face.

She turned to me, her eyes warm, and the tears had nothing to do with earlier, but they were full of happiness.

"I love you," I leaned toward her and kissed her.

"You're ours foreveeerrr," I said, doing a play on her name.

The four of us laid down on the blanket under the night sky and just looked up at it for hours. We were rejoicing in the fact that we had survived. We had been some of the lucky ones. My eyes met Cal's and Matty's, and I smiled at them. This was better than what we had envisioned as kids. They didn't have to say it with their words because I could feel it.

This was the feeling of belonging we had been chasing our whole lives. Everly was the missing piece we had needed.

Tragedy broke you apart, but it had also brought us back together in our case.

EPILOGUE

EVERLY

I couldn't believe we were here. How was this my life? *Our lives?*

Saint and Mateo were on either side of me, all of us with huge smiles on our faces that we couldn't hide.

The plastic chair was uncomfortable beneath me, but I didn't care. We were here to watch Callum graduate. Next year, it would be the turn of me, Mateo, and Saint. But right now, Callum was reaping the rewards of all his hard work.

We watched Callum as he stepped onto the sidelines of the stage after shaking hands with the new dean, a guy that was very much in Lorenzo's pocket. That was a good thing. I didn't necessarily trust Lorenzo, but I knew that he had the best interests of Blackstone in mind.

The names were called, and we watched the graduating students step across the stage. Callum caught my eye from the side and blew me a kiss.

My stomach flipped. I loved these guys so much, and I knew they loved me.

"I'm so fucking proud of Cal." Saint leaned closer to me.

"Yeah. Me too." Mateo nodded. "All of us should be proud."

We should.

There was a long wait until the graduation ceremony was over, and then finally, we were alone.

Just me, Callum, Mateo, and Saint.

My Boneyard Kings.

"I'm so lucky to have you," I whispered to Mateo and Saint, running my hand across the back of the chair I'd been sitting on for the ceremony. I was dimly aware of people clearing chairs away around me, and I rose to my feet. "Please, can we go home?"

Almost as soon as I'd asked the question, we were in the truck.

When we reached the house, the three of them stripped naked and came for me, taking my clothes off in slow increments, worshipping my body, sending me toward the edge before I'd even touched them.

I had no words. This was an experience like no other.

All four of us felt the significance.

"Callum. We're so—" I paused on a gasp as I sank down onto his dick.

"Proud of you," Saint rasped, thrusting up. My ass was so full.

"Ready?" Mateo caught my eye, and I somehow managed to nod, moaning as he pushed his thick cock inside my mouth.

Together, they sent me over the edge, and followed me over.

MATEO

Life after the storm was fucking sweet. Summer was here, and for the first time it meant something. Cal had fucking graduated. He was the first to do it.

"You would've been so proud, old man," I said as I touched his headstone.

I'd like to think he and Erick were reunited in the afterlife. After I made my stop there, I dropped off some flowers for my mother.

I knew Everly or the guys would have liked to come with me and pay their respects, but there was something I needed to do. Something I had never understood until now.

Touching my mother's headstone, I said the words I should have said a long time ago.

"*Te perdono*, Ma."

I forgave her.

I was done holding on to hate. I wanted to start fresh with our girl, and I knew my mother had loved me. Even if it was the wrong kind of love, she had done her best.

My phone started to blow up, and I knew it was Saint's annoying ass telling me to hurry up so we could get to our appointment on time. When I pulled up to the yard, I took a moment to appreciate all the hard work we had done. Slowly, the whole place was getting a lift. It looked more like a home, but it would always be the boneyard to us.

The three of them came out. Everly ran to the car, and then gave me a kiss.

"You disappeared on us," she said.

"Buckle up, mamas, we have a surprise for you."

She narrowed her eyes at all of us.

"How did you guys keep Saint from spilling?" she asked, trying to hide her laughter.

Saint, on the other hand, looked appalled.

"Everrrly," he said. "Do you think I can't keep my mouth shut?"

"She doesn't think, she knows," I said.

Cal laughed then coughed, "No pussy."

Because that was the only way Saint would keep a secret. He flipped us both off and it was nice to know that no matter how much some things changed, others would always stay the same.

Lorenzo had called us last night to let us know that the memorial was now done. When we arrived, we parked across the street because it was still taped off until the inauguration, which would be tomorrow.

He had the workers leave a small space for us to go through. Once I parked the truck, everyone followed. The four of us walked in through the small space, and I instantly knew why Lorenzo had left this area open for us.

We were all speechless.

I knew where Lorenzo had gotten his inspiration from. Plazas Mexicanas. Rows of trees lined a path with benches everywhere. You could hear the chirping of birds and smell the flowers. It was green and filled with color.

"It's so beautiful," Everly whispered.

"Just like you, baby," Saint said, and we all heard when he slapped her ass.

She held on to my hand, and then Cal's.

"You need some self-control," she teased Saint. He pouted but followed right next to us.

When we got to the center, we saw an obsidian fountain. At the top, *Erick Evans Memorial Garden* had been carved, and the words had been filled in with gold. Underneath, it had the names of all the victims.

None of us said a word as we took it all in.

"Everything in life has a purpose," I began to say.

"And that purpose led you to us," Cal finished.

Everly smiled tenderly at us.

Saint turned her around, and here, with the three of us, and Erick's legacy behind us, we gave her a piece of us we had never given anyone else.

"What are you guys doing?" Everly asked as we began to pull our shirts up.

She was going to say more, but instead, she gasped when she saw what we had tattooed above our hearts.

Her hands came out and began to trace the outlines of our tattoos. Keeping this secret from her had been a bitch, but the appreciation on her face was everything.

ForEver, the tattoos read.

And it was simple: for Everly.

She was ours forever.

THE END

THANK YOU

Thank you so much for reading Ruthless Kingdom!

We hope you enjoyed this book, but even if you didn't, reviews are always very appreciated!

Thanks again,

Becca & Claudia

P.S. We will be back!

ABOUT BECCA STEELE

Becca Steele is a USA Today and Wall Street Journal bestselling romance author. She currently lives in the south of England with a whole horde of characters that reside inside her head.

When she's not writing, you can find her reading or watching Netflix, usually with a glass of wine in hand. Failing that, she'll be online hunting for memes, or wasting time making her 500th Spotify playlist.

Join Becca's Facebook reader group Becca's Book Bar, sign up to her mailing list, or visit her website https://authorbeccasteele.com

Other links:

- facebook.com/authorbeccasteele
- instagram.com/authorbeccasteele
- bookbub.com/authors/becca-steele
- goodreads.com/authorbeccasteele
- amazon.com/Becca-Steele/e/B07WT6GWB2

ABOUT C. LYMARI

Claudia lives in the Chicagoland suburbs. When she's not busy chasing after her adorable little spawn, she's fighting with the characters inside her head.

Claudia writes both sweet and dark romances that will give you all the feels. Her other talents include binge watching shows on Netflix and eating all kinds of chips.

Want to know more about me?
  Stay up to date on my Facebook
  Join my Reader Group: Claudia's Coffee Shop
  Instagram account: @C.Lymari
  www.clymaribooks.com

- facebook.com/clymari
- instagram.com/c.lymari
- bookbub.com/authors/c-lymari
- goodreads.com/clymaribooks
- amazon.com/C-Lymari/e/B07VBNT73R

ALSO BY BECCA STEELE

The Four Series

The Lies We Tell

The Secrets We Hide

The Havoc We Wreak

A Cavendish Christmas (free short story)*

The Fight In Us

The Bonds We Break

Alstone High Standalones

Trick Me Twice

Cross the Line (M/M)

In a Week (free short story)*

Savage Rivals (M/M)

London Players Series

The Offer

London Suits Series

The Deal

The Truce

The Wish (a festive short story)*

Other Standalones

Mayhem (a Four series spinoff)*

Boneyard Kings Series (with C. Lymari)

Merciless Kings (RH)

Vicious Queen (RH)

Ruthless Kingdom (RH)

all free short stories and bonus scenes are available from https://authorbeccasteele.com

ALSO BY C. LYMARI

Homecoming Series

It's Not Home Without You - Hoco#1

(Second Chance/ Forbidden)

The Way Back Home - Hoco #2

(Friends-to-Lovers)

You Were Always Home - Hoco #3

(Enemies-to-Lovers/ Second Chances)

HOCO#4- Coming Soon!

(Quincy's & Jessa's story)

Sekten Series

Savage Kingdom

Cruel Crown

(Extremely dark & full of triggers)

Standalones

For Three Seconds

(Forbidden/ Sports Romance)

Falcon's Prey

(A Dark Romance)

In The Midst Of Chaos

(MC Romance)

Swan Song

(Dark Age Gap/Daddy Romance)

Gilded Cage

(Dark Fairytale Retelling)

Boneyard Kings Series (with Becca Steele)

Merciless Kings

Vicious Queen

Ruthless Kingdom

(RH)

Printed in Great Britain
by Amazon